AN
HONEST
DECEIT

GUY MANKOWSKI

Urbane
PUBLICATIONS

urbanepublications.com

First published in Great Britain in 2016
by Urbane Publications Ltd
Suite 3, Brown Europe House, 33/34 Gleaming Wood Drive,
Chatham, Kent ME5 8RZ
Copyright © Guy Mankowski, 2016

A CIP catalogue record for this book is available
from the British Library.

ISBN 978-1-911129-97-4
EPUB 978-1-911129-98-1
MOBI 978-1-911129-99-8

Design and Typeset by Michelle Morgan

Cover by Michelle Morgan

Printed and bound by 4edge Limited, UK

URBANE

urbanepublications.com

"With **An Honest Deceit** Guy Mankowski has invented a new sub-genre in crime fiction. This novel would satisfy even the most discerning reader. I was hooked. I loved it.

For me, what sets the novel apart, is the lens is directed on the 'male' story and in the direct impact on his career when he tries to investigate his daughter's death, which he suspects was no mere accident.

This is an unusual book that, chameleon-like, shifts as the narrative progresses. It is, importantly and primarily, a study of grief, of how two people cope, collide and collapse when they lose their daughter. But it is not bleak; we hear of the journey this relationship takes, from campus meeting to coping with every parent's worst nightmare. This takes us into the educational arena, tense meetings and inquiries, where the fight must be fought for both careers and justice."

RUTH DUGDALL, bestselling author of *The Sacrificial Man* and *Nowhere Girl*

"A mesmerising observation of speaking truth to power. Reminded me of Murakami. Mankowski writes characters that are painfully human and fallible. I finished it in one night."

HANNA JAMESON, CWA shortlisted writer and author of *Something You Are* and *Girl Seven*

"The beauty of this book resides in his actuality, and in the way the author eases the reader into it by choosing to tell the story directly from Ben's perspective. I was increasingly intrigued by the sharp descriptions of the characters that after a few pages take up a life of their own."

DANIELLA QUAGLIA, Huffington Post

Guy Mankowski is a great writer. Great in the sense that he is unafraid to tackle a multiplicity of themes, genres and characters. I have read all of his novels and a lot of his short stories and I am consistently entranced with his ability (and a bit jealous that he's so damn good) - his prose style is lyrical, direct and carefully allows the reader into the story at a pace which makes you want to keep turning the pages, not an easy thing to do at all. An Honest Deceit is yet another tangent from Mankowski. The characters and story are not what I expected, I WANT to tell you what happens - I WANT to reveal details. I loved this book so much I asked my wife to read it and am still asking her each day how far she's got! The intimacy in the dialogue, the moments that make you stop and read a particular sentence again create an experience you feel you are a part of. I really want to talk to someone about this book - like dissecting a film scene by scene. This is Mankowski's best novel yet. A book of emotional intelligence. A courageous leap forward in characterisation. A book that confirms what I've known for ages. He is one of the best young writers in the UK.

DANIEL GOTHARD, bestselling author of *Simon says* and *Reunited*

GUY MANKOWSKI

AN HONEST DECEIT

This novel is dedicated to my parents, Vivienne and Andrew Mankowski, who have been there for me for the best and worst of times.

CONTENTS

PROLOGUE   13

PART ONE   21

PART TWO   63

ACKNOWLEDGEMENTS   251

PROLOGUE

'*MUM, WHERE DO FISH GO in the winter? They're not in the sea any more. I've checked.*'

A small, dark bob pokes out from behind a small rowing dinghy, placed a few feet from the sea. The girl attached to it is lying belly up, as if the ocean has just handed her over to us.

'Mum' does not answer, and so Marine, with her sandy nose, looks me.

'*Daddy, where do fish go in the winter? Mum's not sure. But they're not in the sea any more. I've checked.*'

If I close my eyes, then I am straight back in that moment. Not remembering it, but back in it. When that moment occurred the scene on the beach felt so permanent. Have you ever had moments like that in your own life? When you exist out of time, and feel privileged to be away from the petty concerns of life? As I did in that pale, milky moment, tinged with sand and faint sun. As my five-year-old daughter Marine, on her first visit to the sea, tried to make sense of the foaming, swaying mass in front of her, I experienced such an instant.

I moved from my warm seat on the white sand to watch her take in the morning tide.

That moment still exists at my core. Its soundtrack is the distant clink of boat rigging on an undulating ocean. Its scent is the smell of rubber from speedboats, glistening from a mellow shore. My young family are, at that moment, concerned only with the sand and the subtle pleasures of the August sun. We have no other problems.

That scene has the same texture as all my other memories from that weekend. In it everything is spiced with salty air. The world is slick with brine, and the sea is ready to redden our fragile bodies after a moment of contact. Our family had entered a mythical pact with the surroundings that weekend. The sea promised to take care of us and we, in turn, promised to cherish it.

Marine was ours then. She belonged only to Juliette and I. She was yet to be swept along by forces we could not control. Slender, slim-limbed Marine, in a stripy, blue and white summer dress. That summer, whenever she smiled, she tended to squint, as if overpowered by the sudden happiness of it all. It was the summer that she kept pulling Juliette's hair over her mouth, and laughing at the thought of her mother having a moustache. To answer her question I remember just shrugging. Her head disappeared back behind that small dinghy.

We had left for the beach early that morning. The parts of London that had decamped to the island over summer had been making their way back home over the past few days, and I could not resist wanting to bathe my family in that glacial morning light once more before we left. I remembered it all so vividly from when I was a young boy. The exoticism of the moored boats in the harbour, each laced with the salt of former journeys. The dissolved mysteries of summer.

When I closed my eyes I knew that on opening them, Marine would be there. Right now I want to grasp that feeling so hard that I consume it. I know that in that memory, if I walk just a few yards down the golden incline of the beach, Marine will be hiding behind the dinghy. She will simply be consumed with making a pristine sandcastle, and her eyes will be bedazzled by waves. Sometimes, I like to go back there, because Marine lives in that space. With her essence fully realized, as she works out the secret behaviour of water with her toes.

We had gone to this part of the island to get away from it all for a long weekend by the sea, just the four of us. My father, during his rounded, assured lifetime, had built boats in a large hut on the coast. It seemed right that Marine had such a fascination with the sea, given that my father had dedicated a lifetime to taming it. I'd spent many summers on the island as a child, and had long known that some of the east coast had pale, secluded beaches ideal for a family that wanted to be alone. Juliette hadn't had a holiday in nearly two years, and it showed in the whiteness of her skin. She looked as if she was made of china that weekend.

Juliette and I had worked hard to give our young family a home, and now and then we reminded one another that we should stop and savour it. Juliette always smiled with relief when she heard that. She needed to hear that her tireless work wasn't in vain, and so we agreed. Four days away; I would find us one of those eccentric bed and breakfast cottages by the coast, run by a batty couple who swim in the sea throughout winter.

It isn't easy to return to that beach now. Perhaps because I know that the moment I am there Christian will be two again, and Marine will be five, and nothing will have changed. Marine will be living out her secret games, the rules of which we never understood. I know also I will be reminded of the nonchalant passage of time, and I will still do anything to not be reminded of that.

When I look back to that time, I should remember a glow of perfect happiness. But it isn't that simple. I was young back then, I had just finished university but I already had responsibilities: a family. I had to be able to answer questions, to offer instant solutions, but I lacked the confidence of experience. I had a young partner, who I barely knew. I sometimes wondered if she had secrets that made her even less prepared for the journey ahead than I was. It was this sense of her secrecy, of removal, that had somehow prevented me proposing to her, but I still needed her to help hold this fragile raft of a family together. Somehow I had already realized that I had to treat her very carefully. But I did not yet know why.

Juliette had fallen pregnant with Marine quickly, and we hadn't ever had time to get to know one another before our daughter blossomed in our lives. But Juliette had character, and integrity, and together we got through the transition. We were a couple. But it was only on that cool and melancholy day that we arrived on the island, when we got out of the taxi on the promenade, that I remember feeling for the first time I had been handed a family. They were all mysteries to me. As they remain.

In the evenings we ate at the local sailing club, with friends. It was, in many ways, the last place I would have chosen. It was a small playground for the rich, a place for them to clumsily exchange clumsy boasts after a day of unnecessarily competitive racing. But my father, the man who had built the class of boat they raced, had gained a special status there.

Just before we sat down with the group to eat there was a strange moment. It was one in which I perhaps could have read a blueprint of the troubles ahead, if I were more perceptive. I was looking at a photo of my father with the first yacht he built, which the sailing club kept in a thick glass case by the bar. A beguiling scent of perfume preceded Juliette's approach behind me.

'What are you looking at?' she asked. I realized that I couldn't take my eyes off the picture, in which my father looked remarkably like me. He had a wild thatch of hair and his overalls were covered in oil. But the face was the same.

'A picture of my dad,' I said, turning it towards her. 'Did you know that he wanted me take over his business?' I'd had a few drinks by now, and had to secure the bar for grip. She peered in at the picture. I took in the finely crafted features of her face, as she tucked a lock of hair over her ear. 'Do you ever feel like you have let your parents down?' I asked.

I was not expecting much of a response. Juliette looked up at the chandelier overhead, and as its light blasted over her face, she blinked.

'Are you okay?' I asked. She was silent as two tears traced the shape of her cheekbones. Their route - one to the ear, and one to the floor - was as unexpected as her reaction.

'What did I say?'

She shook her head, her lips smiling in mock dismissal. 'Nothing,' she said. 'Let's leave it, shall we?'

I had only ever met her parents very briefly. I didn't have enough information to ruminate with, and I was too woozy to think straight just then anyway. I shook the incident out of my mind, and got on with the evening.

We ate on the veranda outside of the bar. Our table overlooked a darkened, hushed sea. I remember Juliette's hair illuminating as she leant forwards to pass me a bottle of wine. That evening Juliette only smiled when I asked when we should return to the children, who were enjoying the company of an old friend. A slight smile played at the corners of her mouth as she looked up at me. I could not think what had changed her mood. I realized Juliette was a puzzle, a puzzle which I had now committed a whole lifetime to solving.

The sky was almost pitch black when we bade farewell to our friends. This night had started to reveal its hidden index, the words from its hidden pages whispering around the benches on the sea front. The route ahead was decorated with the detritus of summer. The boats covered in tarpaulins, the shuttered beach shops, the cafes loaded with upturned tables. It all made for a melancholy, charming spectacle.

Juliette and I had a brief walk home, along the promenade and down the small winding lane to our B&B. It sat high above the yawning sea, where the rest of our family would be fast asleep by now. I felt that the evening had belatedly returned Juliette to me, tired and happy, and for the first time a little unwrapped. It was so rare for the two of us to have time alone together for a walk. We so rarely get to linger in the moods we constantly reach for, in our favourite songs and books. So when that flickering moment arrives we try to discipline ourselves to feel at home there.

I remember the way Juliette swung her arms from side to side, almost dancing as she walked. 'Are you happy?' I asked.

'I think I'm as close as I can be,' she said.

I didn't ask what she meant, as I felt satisfied by the way her eyes burnt with some rare desire. That night she embodied all the promises of the young woman I had first met. All her suppressed inclinations were now expressed through her movement, in vibrant colours. The usual subtleties of her mannerisms had grown strong with wine and, I hoped, love. I took her in for one blessed moment – the long curve of her body, the aspirations to better lifestyles captured in her smile. I experienced the inexplicable realization that I would sacrifice a lot to make her happy in the years to come, but that I would also never feel quite convinced that I had succeeded.

I only have one more significant memory of that weekend. Just before we packed the car for the ferry home, Marine insisted we use a spare hour to visit the beach one more time. It was the morning our daughter asked us both that question about the sea. Basking in the white blast of the morning sun, Marine picked up smooth pebbles to treasure when she returned home. She would cherish that weekend her whole life, and nurture the thought of playing on the beach whilst my father's boats watched on. Juliette pulled off her plimsolls and ventured one last time into the sea, alone.

I watched her step into it. Sail-less yachts dipped and rose on silver beams of water. Juliette swam out so far that I wondered if I should shout for her to turn around. The waves became so tall that for a few minutes I couldn't see her small, dark head.

I began to panic. But, as small waves offered a lull, I saw that my she was still swimming to the horizon. She seemed driven by some passion that I had never known, her slim arms chopping the water. Determined. Soon she had disappeared again. The terror rose in me once more. I had lost her. I looked and looked - nothing.

I stood up, and ran to the edge of the water. I could no longer see her amongst the waves. It was only as they eased that I saw Juliette, half-a-mile into the ocean, visible from the waist up. Through a veil of morning mist I could just make out her sleeking her long hair over her head, reveling in her solitude. Far from drowning, Juliette had found a sandbank, and had been standing on it all along. Those large waves were nowhere near her. They had passed around her. She had remained untouched.

AN HONEST DECEIT

PART ONE

ONE

IT'S ONLY NOW that I see how much Juliette has changed, after what we had to survive soon after that weekend. As young people, neither her nor I seemed to outwardly possess any toughness, but she was certainly the more fragile of the two of us. I know I have changed too; it's just that I prefer not to consider what I might have become.

The Juliette I first met was a closed book. Although she was yet to come into focus, certain edges of her were creeping to the fore. When I remember her, I see someone who is yet to step out of her own darkness.

Juliette and I were at the same college at university. On the afternoon my dad drove me to my new home I was enchanted. Enchanted by the silver, winding rivers and cobbled streets of that city, the roads that wound past illuminated windows, each of which contained entrancing silhouettes, flitting amongst one another. We drove past immaculate grass lawns, on which vinyl-haired women carried paperbacks. It seemed to like the Promised Land. Though only I had promised it to myself.

I had been brought up in the sticks, in a village so remote that I had never experienced the bustle of a city. I had become so crushingly familiar with the place that I knew the intricacies of each street, each shop, and each corner. I'd notice the moment some aspect of it was altered, and in noticing such tiny details I then felt suffocated. I had sometimes wondered if I was the protagonist in some 70's sci-fi series, in which a man can't escape the confines of his hometown, no matter how hard he tries. I wasn't just desperate to get out, I was as uncultured as the most awkward country bumpkin, and I wanted to remedy that before my new peers realized it was the case. I had never been to see a band play, never had a girlfriend, and had never experimented with anything other than sleep deprivation caused by adolescent worry.

I was studying English Literature, simply because it was the only subject in which I had gained even a decent grade at school. I was captivated by the contents of books at that age. During my last year at school I realized that the more I immersed myself in books, the less I had to worry about the outside world.

Our college had an air of functionality about it, with its sturdy apartment blocks and symmetrical plazas. When I first laid eyes on Juliette it was in the refectory. It was a lunchtime in the first term. I was sat on the table opposite hers, eating with some new acquaintances from my floor. They were debating the merits of a Harold Pinter production that they'd seen the day before. I barely understood a word they were saying.

Juliette had her head down, and she was static in the midst of three girlfriends, each of whom were chatting animated. Juliette's attention was completely consumed by a crumpled piece of paper in her hands, which she was looking at with great concern. So much so, that when her friends rose as one to fetch coffee Juliette stayed fixed to her seat. She only stirred when a friend caught her arm. She looked up. Rich dark curls framed a face that seemed almost too dramatic. I had never seen such a fragile expression, and yet her more assertive friends seemed to fuss around her as if she was one of their own. I must have smiled at her, because she smiled back, with what looked like relief. I remember hoping that I looked sympathetic to whatever plight was occupying her. But I suppose I must have done, because when I joined the queue behind her for a drink she looked back at me, and tucked her hair behind one ear with a vague smile. All this was enough to encourage me. In my inexperienced mind, this very English exchange of polite glances was a passionate tango, a roll in the hay - a spontaneous dance in a summer meadow.

I can't describe the extent to which, at that age, I found women exotic. Juliette's friends were no exception. After they returned, as one, to sip from steaming cups at their table, I noticed how they all had powder blue or scarlet winter coats. Strangely enough, it wasn't their appearances which intrigued me; it was the way they approached their work. As I sipped my drink, and let my new friend gas uninterrupted, they each took out their books. For me, study was an obligation, the rough end of a pact that also offered me some freedom. To these women, university seemed a very serious opportunity, something to be grasped with both hands. I found their combination of discipline and femininity beguiling. At that time, all the possible apparatus that came with woman - from pashmina's to lip-gloss - seemed enticingly foreign.

My roommate, Phillip, gave me a hard time about all this. When I arrived back Phillip was lying on his bed, a vampish woman with wild long hair wrapping her legs around him from behind. His Morrissey quiff quivered as he raised a hand to greet me. 'Maria,' he said, looking round at her, 'Ben's here. If you ever need someone to worry on your behalf, Maria, this is the man. Look at him, he's even worrying about what I meant by that.'

Maria waved an elegant hand. As I placed my rucksack on the table he addressed her with a stage-whisper. 'You want to get some pastries?' he asked her. 'A few Danish, a little Mochaccino?' She shook her head, smiling coquettishly. 'What about some cranberry juice? Top up those fluids?'

I sighed at the showing off.

'All work and no play makes Ben a dull boy,' he announced. 'Now, why don't you come with us to the patisserie?' he asked.

'Because I've got to work, Phil. I don't have time to pretend I'm a 19th century French aristocrat.'

Phillip sat up straight, as Maria began lacing up her heels.

'He's tetchy,' he said, to her. 'Probably something to do with the girl I saw him spying on in the refectory.'

Maria smiled.

'You saw that?' I asked.

'I saw the lot. It was like watching a dog try to mount a railing.'

'What do you mean?'

'You tell me what happened, then I'll tell you what I mean.'

I related to him the story of 'my glance'. As I spoke Maria noisily gathered her possessions and he tried on three different types of boots. As she left he threw on a scarf, lit a cigarette, and blew a plume of smoke through the crack at our window.

'She's a twin,' he said, as Maria closed the door. 'I had a little kissy kissy incident with her sister in the cloak room at the JCR. I thought I was bumping into her a second time but in fact it was Maria. We get on much better though, you know? I think it's to do with her being a linguist. She speaks Serbo-Croat. We're going for cocktails later and her brother has a Hummer.'

'Good for you,' I said. 'That's great.'

'It's going to make hanging out at the student union a problem,' he said. 'I can't tell them apart. One speaks French but besides that you can't slide a playing card between them. It's all about the man making bold moves though, isn't it?'

'You talking about my situation now?'

'Maybe I'm talking about both situations. Either way, you need to be dashing.'

'What does that mean? You want me to buy a tuxedo?'

'No tuxedo,' he said. 'You don't have the shoulders. But next time you see her you need to be bold, because any more staring and she'll have you down as an Engleby in the making.'

It was a bright sunny day just before the Easter holidays, and the still-nameless Juliette was sitting reading by the hockey pitch, as the team ran through their motions. I started thinking about Phillip's typically confusing advice. I wondered how I could I be dashing by a hockey pitch. She didn't appear to be in any danger - I couldn't rescue her. But I knew I had to say something. I had a book under my arm, and I wondered if that would help. I sat on the other side of the bench she was on.

She smiled at me, almost dismissively. But in that fleeting expression I saw something retained in her eyes.

'Have you had the same thought as me?' I asked. 'That this might actually be the quietest place to study?'

'No,' she laughed. 'This is somewhere I can come to stop thinking about my books.'

'Except the one you're reading right now?'

She looked down and smiled. I laughed in return. I wondered if this is what dating would entail: a constant exchange of dry laughs. She lifted the book. It was *Wuthering Heights*.

'Have you read it?' she said.

'I'm afraid not. I'm doing an English Literature course, and I've started to see all reading as work.'

'English Literature! I'm so jealous. You do know that's not work, don't you?'

'It must be, because it's all I do. Look at how pale I am!' I said, pulling my forearms out of my shirt.

'You are indeed,' she said. 'I think I've been spending too much time in on my own as well.'

'Exams?'

'I've started painting,' she said, closing her book and turning to me. As she looked down at her hands I noticed the precision of her features. Sun was coming through the trees behind the pitch, making the hockey players into flashing silhouettes. Juliette's flawless, too-white skin became a fine canvas for those sunbeams.

'Landscapes?'

She shook her head. 'People.'

'People that you know?'

'Sometimes,' she said. 'Sometimes, people I want to remember.'

I didn't know what to say, and it was agonizing to let the moment slip through my fingers.

'So are you locking yourself in your room for fear of being found out, and thrown out of here?' she asked.

'Exactly,' I said, exhaling. 'How did you know that?'

'Because I get that feeling all the time,' she said.

'It's good to meet someone I have that in common with,' I said.

Phillip was elated by the news of this undeniable flirtation, and he paced around our room like a matador as we contemplated what I should do with Juliette's phone number.

'How can I call her?' I said, hunching in the chair at my desk. 'I don't think I can call her.'

'You are not a eunuch,' he said.

I looked up. 'You what?'

He pointed his two cigarette-clenching fingers at me. 'Ben - look at me. You are not a eunuch.'

'I know I'm not a eunuch, Phillip.'

He slouched by the windowsill.

'It's just, I see the situation here,' he said. 'You're a virgin, right? You haven't had your end away, but that's no reason to give up. Just because it hasn't happened, Ben, doesn't mean it won't, okay?'

'Yeah. Sure.'

'But I need you to believe, in your heart, and stop thinking like that.'

'I'm not thinking like that. I'm thinking my roommate needs … to stop calling me a eunuch.'

'Maybe I should talk to her,' he said, peering at me from the side of his eyes. 'You know, maybe I should bump into her and ask her out for you? Lay the groundwork. Tell her about my roommate who's *not* a virgin and she'll go 'Who's this playboy he's talking about?' and then when I mention your name she'll think 'wow, this Ben sounds like a proper Casanova. Then we have her under our thumb.'

'No, Phillip. Don't do that. That doesn't even make sense.'

'You're worried you'll ask her out and she'll say no and you'll get burnt. But you gain respect, as a man, if you get your fingers singed. It's humble, it's beautiful.'

'So I ask her out?'

'Yeah. So we know she likes art,' he said. 'You should get her a ticket to the Egon Schiele exhibition,' he said. 'I can score a couple through the radio station. You can argue that they're free, so it won't even look like you've made any effort.'

'Women don't like you to make an effort?' I asked.

'Sometimes this is like trying to get Pinocchio to act like a real boy. So they want you to make an effort, Ben, but they certainly don't want it to look like you're making an effort,' he said, putting his hands on his hips. 'Trust me on this. Call her.'

'I don't know anything about Egon Schiele,' I said. 'I could get a book out?'

He laughed, and stubbed out the cigarette.

When I phoned the number she'd given me I expected no one on her hall to answer it. The voice that did pick up told me to hang on. I listened to a low buzz of static for two minutes. When Juliette did answer, she seemed surprised to have a caller.

'Ben? I didn't expect you to ring.'

'Why not?'

'I don't know.'

'Well, I remembered that you mentioned painting. I've scored us a couple of tickets to the Egon Schiele exhibition - it's in the campus art gallery and with you painting people -'

I tried to remember the lines I had practised. They sounded woolly now.

'Yeah, I know about it,' she said.

I didn't think for a moment that her curt response might be a result of her shyness. I assumed she was weighing up her options, mentally comparing me to the droves of other men that had asked her out that week.

'I thought you might be interested.'

'That sounds like fun,' she said. 'When shall we do it?'

Three days later was my first date, with the future mother of my children. In the pages of my life, this day would be one I would return to read again and again.

Perhaps I am merely viewing the date through the romantic shroud of the past, but winter seemed to move in more quickly then. One morning I awoke to find the grass outside my bedroom window covered in an icy sheen. The air had a clean, glacial feel. I spent hours inspecting my skin before the date, convinced that a spot I hadn't noticed would permanently disgust her. In the end I decided it was more important to be on time.

As I walked to meet Juliette I noticed the square outside the university art gallery had become an ice rink. Bing Crosby was singing Jingle Bells from hidden speakers, the melody ringing clearly in the bright air. His warm tones were interspersed with the sounds of distant blades cutting the surface. Through the mist rising off the ice it looked like fireflies, wrapped in cotton wool, were circling each other as they skated. As I walked closer, the translucent sheet of ice reflected the imperious, neoclassical green dome of the library overlooking the rink. The library's twin pillars were adorned with long adverts for the exhibition, which made it look as though two emaciated sketches were watching over the events beneath them. I suddenly had the sense that life was preparing a cushion for me, as I was soon going to fall into something. I looked for Juliette amongst the upturned collars and bright scarves.

When I found her, watching the skaters from the side of the rink, I was struck by how precise she looked. Her dark curls poured over the fake fur of her lapels. As she turned to look at me I saw that her features were chilled by the wind, and her lips were sparkling. She turned to hug me and as I received her I dared not hold her for too long, for fear that I would betray something. I realized I had no idea what to say, or what to do with her.

'I'm so excited to finally see this exhibition,' she said, as we moved inside. 'I've wanted to go for a long time.'

'Then why didn't you?' I asked.

She seemed amused. 'I don't know.' She looked at me, as if anticipating my reaction to her next remark. 'My dad used to say exhibitions were a waste of time, just a way for some show-off to fleece the public of their money. I felt daft coming by myself, like I didn't have permission or something.'

'Well you can forget about him,' I said. 'Because you now have my permission.'

She smiled. I got our tickets out and showed her them. 'I mean, I've bought them now,' I said, waving them in the air. 'So it would be too late to turn back even if you weren't interested.' Her smile turned to a laugh.

The exhibition looked full, judging from the mass of bodies pushing to get into the entrance. People sidled into the gap between two white walls, 'Egon Schiele' stencilled in bold black on the right hand side. Eager, lithe students mixed with the more cautious, discerning gallery goers shakily consulting leaflets. As we moved through the four small rooms I realized how ignorant I was about art, and about the protocol of a date. I had anticipated feeling this way and Phillip had told me, in this circumstance to just 'do what I wanted, and act confident'.

Juliette's shyness seemed to vanish when she began to talk about the art. 'His muse was often his sister, Gertie,' she whispered. 'He often painted her in a way that was considered pretty lewd.' She stopped in front of one portrait.

'Why do you think he looked at her like that?' I asked, looking at the picture. In it, Gertie's hands were sinewy, and she was pushing them towards the viewer.

'I just think he painted what he saw,' she said, stepping gently into a reverie that was sudden and beautiful. I wished I could enter its porous boundaries, be enveloped in its unique texture. 'Women aren't just the soft, dreamy muses that most artists paint them as,' she said. 'He wasn't afraid to represent that. Which I like.' Her cheeks had warmed into a rosy glow.

'Has he inspired you?' I asked.

'I suppose so,' she said.

Her scent enshrouded me, drawing me closer to the fabric of her arm. I realized that her fingers were lightly placed on the crook of my elbow, as if we were guiding one another. It sounds so incidental, but it took some courage for me to allow us to keep touching one another. It felt intimate, to be caught in the tendrils of the next movement of her mind and body.

Afterwards, as we moved towards the cloakroom, I said, 'I'd love to see your paintings. What do other people think of them?'

She moved forward to retrieve her coat from the attendant.

'You're the only one that knows they exist,' she said. She looked behind at me for a second, and smiled.

I took a mental polaroid of that instant, which I carry in my mind. At that moment I told myself that Juliette could not have smiled at me in that way if she did not think we could fall in love.

TWO

WHEN I DECIDED to become a teacher, I didn't think for a second I would end up famous. I thought teaching was a way to stay out of the limelight.

I first learnt that shy people shouldn't be teachers, just after I gained my PGCE. I was sent to a special-measures school where the children were bigger, louder and more confident than I'd ever been. Somehow I learnt to quell my racing heart, my dry mouth, and ignore the sudden bloom of sweat that arose in my armpits whenever I needed to begin a class. During that part of your career, you do not believe that you can alter the world. Your sense of possibility is shaped by the sentiments offered by your supervisors, and the room they offer you to flourish in. I became a teacher because I wanted to help children overcome their shyness.

Much to my surprise, I enjoyed a job that forced me to leave my ego at the door. I found myself developing odd little strategies that helped me connect with the children, which helped me to enjoy teaching them. With the younger children I'd often use different voices, and these sudden about-turns would amuse and engage them. With the older children I learnt when to push and when to withdraw slightly, and in so doing how to bring them out of the shell. Gradually, I saw the classroom as less an arena of fear and more a den of possibility.

I had been teaching high school students, at a school called Cranley Wood, for a few months when this situation changed. I had been working under a diligent headmistress who was firm, but who clearly enjoyed running the school. I heard by email, on a wet Wednesday afternoon, that she was retiring and that she would be replaced by an 'exciting, visionary' headmaster called Paul Kraver. I wondered who would have written that, and decided it was Kraver's voice we were hearing. The email added that he would not only lead this school but also its nearby affiliates.

I had spoken to the headmistress only days before, watching my breath form in the cold while she smoked a cigarette, and she had told me her ambitions for the school. I wondered what had changed so quickly. A few hours later a terse email from Kraver told us all to be in the common room an hour early, the following Friday.

In the intervening days dark rumours circled. The school became a foreboding place, where tempers frayed. I overheard a number of shouting matches, too distant to comprehend. A number of the older staff were sure they were about to be made redundant. During spiky exchanges in the common room one or two indulgently remarked that they wanted to leave, rather than some amateur lead them. But when some newer members of staff were told they were being forced to leave, the feigned acquiesce turned into something more hostile. I wondered if I would fall victim to a 'last in, first out' policy, and be back to square one in my career. Pupils became openly upset, complaining in classes about how they would soon lose a favourite teacher. The staff speculated that Paul Kraver had only got the job through a friend at the council, who would be the real puppet master behind the job, and that a slew of redundancies would help fund his reputedly enormous salary. But despite the strength of the fear no one was able to find out much about our new leader. We waited for Friday, exchanging scraps of half-verified information in the run-up.

Early that morning I sat in an anxious semi-circle of sleep-deprived staff, in the common room, and we waited Kraver to make an appearance. The common room was, at the best of times, too small for us. It actually fostered a sense of community, as we didn't have enough space to avoid each other. But today the room was full - the tatty chairs at the lunch tables all occupied, with some staff members even having to resort to sitting on the windowsill. Our deputy headmaster, James, was washing up and telling everyone that Kraver wasn't the usual, harried headmaster we were probably expecting. 'I read online that he's a media graduate, who somehow ended up running a private health care company,' he said, suds flying into his hipster beard.

'How does that qualify him to run a school, then?' said the school nurse, sponging the cups with a towel.

'Because it isn't just a school now, is it? Not since the new government. It's a franchise. A money-making venture. There'll be targets to meet. And if they're met, money will pour in. Then one day, it'll turn private. It'll be pay day for everyone - except us.'

The school had recently merged with a primary school over the road, and both were now functioning under the title 'Cranley Wood'. There had been quite a stir about this development in the community. This high school had, over the years, developed quite a reputation for being rough, with a few nasty incidents involving drugs and knives. But the primary school was known for being a most pleasant place. The rumour was that, following the merger, once the reputation of our school had improved this would be exploited by it charging high fees. There was a third campus being incorporated under the banner too - a sixth form college called The Eden Site, which was had just been built. The beginnings of an empire. Which this Kraver would seemingly run.

'As long as the kids don't stop getting sick,' said the school nurse, hanging the cups onto small hooks, 'and I have a job, I'm all for change.'

'Change is good,' said Kraver as he appeared in the doorway.

James dropped a mug into the water, with a soft plop.

Kraver stood in the doorway. He was a rotund man, whose belly bulged from under the type of multi-coloured waistcoat favoured by eighties snooker players. He was balding, though it was his broad smile that was first apparent, and it revealed that he enjoyed the theatre surrounding his arrival. It also revealed two sharp, rather yellow incisors, which somehow glinted in the light.

'Well, well, well, look at you all,' he said, arms folded behind his back, walking back and forth in front of the crescent of chairs as if we were Royal Marines.

A brilliant bunch of front line soldiers we'd have made. Me, blissfully ignorant of a large chilli stain on my shirt, which I would only learn the existence of when Tobias Channing in 10D pointed it out later on that day. Ruth Unsworth, who sat next to me, had perfected the art of neurotic knitting, that reached a crescendo of clacking as Kraver spoke. Colin McGregor, the barrel-chested PE teacher, was bouncing a basketball clumsily on the floor. I couldn't help but notice all the other members of staff straightening their backs as Kraver found his groove.

'You can all exhale now.' He put his thumbs in his waistcoat pocket. 'I might look like I've eaten one of you for breakfast, but I promise I won't.'

Some nervous titters.

'Righteo,' Kraver continued, 'The best way to start is for me to let you know my policy. How I run a place, right? What I do, is, I begin with a splash.' His hands waved in the air, and he mimed droplets falling on us. Colin pretended to wipe one from his brow.

'Now, it's no secret that this school is known as being the roughest in the district. Maybe even in the county, am I right?'

The question was rhetorical.

'Last year, you just about managed to claw your way out of Special Measures. Very good. But I want to do much more. I want parents to be fighting to get their kids in here. And how will I do that, I hear you ask? By showing off to the world the virtues of this place. So, I have decided in my first act as your new headmaster, to let camera crews come in as part of a new TV programme called "Educating Bristol".'

A ripple of shock passed through the room.

'I'd better get my hair done,' Ruth said, setting down her needles.

Kraver nodded, pleased at the reaction. 'This fine place, Cranley Wood, is going to swagger into the public eye.'

'Are you sure that's wise?' Colin muttered.

'We shall take the risk,' he said, addressing him. The hands came out of the pockets as he started to wag his finger. 'Every day is a gamble, isn't it, am I right? You might pull the rabbit out of the hat, or it might stay firmly hidden in there. What I'm saying is, that from today, we up the stakes. We have nothing to hide, and everything to be proud of.'

'How do you know, you've just got 'ere?' the nurse murmured, touching my shoulder.

Kraver swiveled to look at her. It was a remark that I had thought cheeky at best. But Kraver widened his eyes at her, and her reaction suggested that it felt like a blast of white heat had hit her face. 'You don't want to question me,' Kraver said. 'Unless you have something to hide. I'm sure you have nothing to hide, do you?'

The nurse seemed to shrink in her uniform.

'So - no questions, and everyone best of friends. Wonderful and tremendous. All is well on board the good ship Cranley Wood.'

'You sure about that?' Ruth asked, as laughter from outside pierced through. 'Even 6F?'

'Ruth, you talk of 6F as if they're a small division of the English Defence League,' Colin said. 'They're not that bad.'

A few people laughed. It eased the pressure in the tightened air.

'You try teaching them after they've been in the rain,' she answered, poking a needle at him. 'It's a fight to prevent the vainer boys from going topless and putting their shirts on the radiators. Alice Jenkins nearly had a stroke when Rob Makin showed her his nipples. How's that going to look on primetime Channel 4?'

Colin turned to me.

'Talking of behaviour during rubbish weather, what about Ben's habit of encouraging students to throw snowballs at teachers?'

This roused a cheer. 'He's got you there, Ben,' James said.

'I only did that once, because they were throwing snowballs at you, Colin,' I answered.

'And weren't you letting them do that in exchange for them coming inside quickly?' Ruth asked.

'You're absolutely right, Mrs. Unsworth,' I said, cautious. 'I was letting them paste Colin with slushy balls for the good of their own education.'

'I see,' Kraver said, eyeballing me with an intense stare. 'A good school is a fun place to be. They will capture us at our ducking and diving best, delivering day after day, come rain, shine, or slushy snowballs. You watch. Things are going to change around here.' He wagged a stubby finger. 'Make no mistake.'

I wasn't sure what to make of Kraver. Later that day, in the school corridor, I saw a small crowd of younger pupils had gathered around him as he performed card tricks. Whilst the cooler girls in the sixth form watched, arms folded, the younger ones seemed impressed. 'Show us how you did that,' one said. Kraver addressed one of the sixth form girls. 'Some secrets are more fun if they're kept, aren't they girls?' he said.

'I bet he can make my salary disappear, no problem,' Colin said, hovering behind me.

'Hmm,' I said, watching the girls consult, trying to discern what they thought of their new head.

'There's a hint of The Magic Circle about him. Isn't there?' Colin said.

I watched Kraver as he moved through the door and outside into the playground. His peculiar, shuffling walk seemed to betray that he had spotted something outside, but to my eye the yard was clear. I waited, and a few moments later I was surprised to see a young boy walking in front of him, his head down, on his way back to class. I tried to catch what Kraver was saying to him through the glass, but only caught the tail end of it as the boy opened the door.

'Or, you can continue to rile me and I'll make your life a living hell,' he was saying.

The boy, his face white, hurried to class. Kraver looked up at me. 'Got to keep them on their toes, eh?' he said.

Juliette had less concerns about the ongoing privatization, and decided that Marine should stay at the affiliated school over the road, with Christian. Making ends meet with two children wasn't easy, but my main concern was putting food on the table. So once the new regime started I just focused on getting on with my life, and I very rarely noticed the cameras that had begun to become a feature of every school corridor.

When the programme finally aired, its viewing figures were so big it came second only to The X Factor in the Saturday night ratings. People kept asking me if, in the scenes I was featured in, I was playing up to the camera. The question was leveled at me more and more frequently as the season went on. I caught one or two episodes but didn't really enjoy seeing my harried face on a TV screen during my few hours off. As far as I was concerned, I was just a bloke trying to inspire a struggling class to get through their GCSEs.

It was only after some of my teaching methods were shown on national television that I realized how eccentric they were. I'd thought a lot of them were just necessary strategies to get the pupils onboard. But once Colin showed me them, in YouTube clips which had over a million hits, I began to understand what the fuss was all about.

In the first episode I was shown catching a wayward student, Aaliyah, writing a large phallic symbol and the words 'Cranley Wood is pretty shite' in black marker pen on a bench. So I gave her the choice of being in after-school detention, or taking my advice and using felt tips from the art department to alter the graffiti to something positive. Kraver admonished me for encouraging graffiti, but after Aaliyah had converted the phallus to a bunch of flowers, and changed the aforementioned slogan to the words 'Crawley Wood is a pretty s i lky smooth place to be' he reluctantly decided to praise me. The school caretaker, Morris, patted me on the back too. I'd saved him an afternoon of painting, and he said he'd buy me a pint.

In the next episode I caught a student selling controversial computer games to Year 10s. A couple of the more notable titles included 'Bikini Samurai IV' and 'Halloween Booby Trap III'. A YouTube clip quickly appeared, in which I speculated with Colin, over a cup of Earl Grey, exactly what the storyline of Halloween Booby Trap might be. I wondered if in the game any boobies literally got trapped? Was there a booby prize at the end of each level? A few other members of staff joined in the riff, and to make the situation even more absurd I ended up planning, on the whiteboard, a staff tournament where the person who got furthest on Halloween Booby Trap bought a round at the pub at the next staff do. Once the video reached a million hits I realized that my fellow staff members weren't just laughing out of kindness.

But the reason I became famous overnight (or as Phillip described it 'a shoe-in for the next series of Celebrity Apprentice') wasn't just because of such tomfoolery.

A student in my class, Marie, was left abandoned by her single mother when she departed for a summer job in Tenerife. Marie been bounced around various relatives up to the start of the academic near and the poor girl was having to divide her time between her grandparents' house and a pretty rough local foster home. Marie was determined not to follow in the footsteps of her mother and fall pregnant as a teenager. She had gone from being a bit of a troublemaker when she first joined the school (she was briefly suspended for having too many facial piercings) to gradually deciding that she wanted to get the qualifications to go to college.

The fifth episode of 'Educating Bristol' followed a conversation I had with her in after-school detention. As punishment for stealing from the canteen I'd asked her to write out her ambitions.

Before letting Marie go, I distractedly asked her if she wanted to read out what she had written. I'll never forget how Marie, in a voice that was at once faltering and determined, read out her piece.

It opened with a description of the midwife that saved her mother's life during her premature birth. With one hand on her hip, Marie told the detention that she was named after that midwife, who was now her heroine. As she related the story, I was struck by the change in this complex young lady. Schoolchildren are usually very cautious about sharing personal details of their life, and in my experience they are understandably wary of making themselves appear vulnerable in front of their peers. But as Marie read, a steeliness came into her voice which made the others sit up straight (no mean feat for a room full of students who'd offered little evidence that they owned a functioning spine in my class). Her mother, Marie said, described that midwife as one of the few people who had 'made a difference' in her life. As she neared the end she put the piece of paper on a table. 'I'm going to pass my GCSEs, and sit for 'A' Levels,' she announced. 'I'm going to go to college, train to be a midwife, and make my mum proud of me. I think it is the only way to bring her home,' she said, her voice breaking at the end of the sentence.

I was amazed at the transformation. 'That's a beautiful piece of writing, Marie,' I said. I motioned for her to sit down, and at this point in the programme the camera zoomed in on the shocked faces of the boys watching for her next statement.

'You have a very commendable sense of ambition, Marie,' I said. 'I tell you, if you learn to channel that ambition there is no reason why you can't achieve your goal.'

'University?' one of the boys scoffed. 'But Marie thinks hummus is a place in Palestine.'

'Do you want to have his attitude towards life, or do you want to be like the midwife that saved your mother's life?' I asked Marie.

'The midwife,' she answered.

'Complete your homework to the highest standard you can, Marie. Keep yourself focused in class, and hold onto that feeling you had when you read out that piece,' I said, patting my hand on my heart. 'I guarantee, if you do that, no one will stop you getting into college. The question is, can you start doing all that *right now*? Because I am afraid you have no more time to waste.'

'Yes sir,' Marie said.

'Then I'll make a deal with you,' I answered. 'You get seven GCSEs from A-C, and I will stand up in front of the whole school in assembly dressed in the kind of outfit this midwife must have to wear every day,' I said.

'You mean a nurses' outfit?' Marie said, clapping her hands to her face.

The boys behind her guffawed. 'Always knew sir was a bender,' one said.

I decided to let that slide.

Marie didn't need any more motivation. I like to think that the thought of me making a fool of myself in front of the whole school spurred her on. Perhaps I hadn't thought through how I would feel when my parents saw me, on national TV, address a packed school assembly bursting out of a skin-tight nurses' outfit. But I like to think that my embarrassment made Marie enjoy her eventual success all the more. Either way, I finally felt that I had become an educator. I could see no reason why life wouldn't be smooth sailing from now on.

THREE

IN OUR HOME, we blocked out Daddy being on television every week. As a family we had no idea how well-known I was becoming, or would that would lead to. Marine had turned ten and now Christian had been at school for a couple of years Juliette was at last starting to find her feet in her own career again. Christian was proving to be less of a handful than Marine and for the first time it looked as though Juliette might be able to focus on her own career.

It was a relief to us that Marine had, at last become less of a constant challenge. When we had first become parents getting Marine to sleep had been almost impossible. I tried every trick in the parenting manual, and none of them seemed to work on the energetic scribble of energy that was our daughter. With her eyes red from tiredness, Juliette would drag herself into Marine's bedroom. She'd cradle her daughter with a tenderness that seemed almost excessive. Juliette would sit, visible only by the faint luminescence of a white plastic moon chandelier, and rock Marine in her arms whilst singing the words to '*Au Clare De*

La Lune'. '*Under the Moonlight*' was the traditional French song Juliette's grandmother had sung to her, and it became to Marine something of a lullaby. Often she would only fall asleep once her mother had sang it to her a few times, each rendition more weary than the last. Perhaps it is because I only ever heard that song in states of extreme tiredness, but its lilting, Gallic melody weaved its way deep into my subconscious. As my mind drifted in and out of a sleep I craved, often the thread that connected my dreams was Juliette's voice, fragile and a little flat, with that distinctive French edge. That melody is now a part of my dreamscape, and it's a melody that often returns to me when I'm at a low ebb.

By the time 'Educating Bristol' aired Juliette had relaxed into being a mother. We now had new pleasures revealed to us - the pleasures of being a family unit with its own, unique strategies on handling life. Of course, like any family, our strategy was usually 'to make do and mend'. Like all young couples, Juliette and I had had that hairy period in which, in rented flats with two young children, we'd quickly learnt to fit around each other. I liked to stay up with a cold beer, but Juliette liked to just sleep when the children would let her, and we grumpily worked towards compromises. We both jumped from short-term job to short-term job - me as a trainee teacher, and her as an architect's assistant, trying to save the money to buy our own place. When we eventually bought our house the electrics and plumbing were a mess, and we weathered the storm of broken boilers and frosty mornings until we had saved more money to fix the place. I learnt, not only during childbirth, but also during this time, that Juliette was stoical, tougher than her beautiful exterior might have suggested. Once the home was habitable, Juliette tastefully decorated our new house. The wood-panelled floors and low, beamed ceilings framed a chic, homely environment that often chimed with the excited voices of our children.

Any Englishman needs his castle, and in my mind the creaky steps up to our first floor home were a kind of moat strangers had to overcome before they could reach my family. Though we owned the ground floor, we rented it to a student couple to help us afford the mortgage. I finally felt as if my family was safe in our little nest, and I looked forward to the day when we had enough money to have a whole house to ourselves.

Juliette also finally had the space to paint. The light from the street outside would fall onto the corner of our living room where she worked. That golden shaft was often dappled with the shapes of flickering leaves from the oak tree opposite. I would return home to see that Juliette had propped an easel up close to the window, and covered an old coffee table in drying paints in preparation. But it was Marine who inspired her to actually begin painting.

Marine never stopped moving. She recited, word for word, her favorite television shows. She asked old women in the street why they had moustaches, and did so with enough charm that she wasn't hit. She asked bus drivers why they didn't look happy. She got the shy children at school to join in the games she had invented. Games with complex storylines and characters. But it wasn't only children that Marine brought out of their shell. Her energy, her lust for life, her ability to speak the unspoken all invigorated Juliette.

After a few weeks finished canvases started to build in a pile under the window. In every one of them Juliette had captured Marine - playing, jumping, sprawling.

When Juliette painted Marine, she did so with blazing gold, darting orange, and vivid red. I watched her frenetically paint one afternoon, Marine toying with a farm set beneath her, as she threw colours across the canvas. In this fitful burst of creativity Juliette's red satin dress fell around her elbows. A lattice of dark hair obscured one side of her face. Juliette was never more alive than when she was painting her daughter.

Phillip had moved onto a nearby street with his girlfriend Christine. He had recently completed a stand-up tour which had seen him win awards at The Edinburgh Fringe. It seemed remarkable that Phillip's professional career bloomed at the same time he met his partner-in-crime. During a dinner at ours, Phillip's usual stories about uncompromising positions he'd ended up in were less frequent. He now concerned himself with attending to Christine's every wish, taking her stylish wrap from her shoulders, offering to top up her wine, and encouraging her to tell us about her sculpting. He only revealed his true former ebullience in a spiky anecdote about media types he'd recently met. Christine's poised interjections seemed to keep Phillip on a leash, and I think he had finally realized that he needed that. I decided that Christine's louche demeanor concealed a secret lack of confidence, permitting her to only speak when she was sure of her remarks. On the occasions that I saw Phillip and Christine together they were even wearing the same colours.

Marine had inherited her mother's love of art, and her brightly coloured daubings illuminated many surfaces of the house. But her exuberance wasn't only limited to her pictures. Her primary school teacher, an aquiline blonde called Katy Fergus, would occasionally contact us with news of the rather unusual ways Marine had drawn attention to herself in class. On the parents' evenings where I met Katy she would describe the latest incident, in a voice that sounded at once charmed and increasingly panicked.

There was the sewing lesson when Marine swallowed a large bead, then convinced two of her friends to do the same, as it was 'a pill that would make them fly'. I had to negotiate my way through some fraught phone calls with some distressed parents after that.

Marine told the other children vivid stories about a moaning ghost that rose from under their beds if they didn't sleep, ensuring insomnia in various homes. Marine's teenage years were a long way away, but I couldn't help dreading what kind of an adolescent she would become.

It was early summer when I decided to start to take Marine out on my own. A clutch of new fairgrounds had opened on the nearby coast. As we walked into the array of flashing lights, whirling rides and neon candy, Marine's eyes danced. All around us roller coasters clacked and cornered; hot dog stands sizzled and spat. Marine's excitement entranced me. I started to see the world as a playground, a heady mix of colourful pleasures.

She insisted we shoot pellets at the Rootin' Tootin' shooting range, where a direct hit on a bobbing Indian could earn you a fluffy Simba. While we were playing, I completely bought into the tiny world that each ride created. With Marine next to me I could almost believe I was hunting for Indians in The Wild West. That the 'Snake of Death' (a tunnel slide about fifteen feet high) really did defy the boundaries of mortality, or that a direct hit from another dodgem might be the end of us. When we rode the dodgems Marine implored me to avoid the impact of other cars, but she collapsed in giggles when someone hit us. She flung her hands into the air when the buzzer signaled the end of the ride, and leapt from the car like a cowboy off a horse. Marine threw herself into every ride, sang along with every melody, and shot her way to victory on every gala.

She liked the dark arcade booths most children would have been scared of. I had to gently usher her away from the likes of Terminator 2, in favour of Star Wars. As we entered that booth together I felt like we were entering a dark universe, as father and daughter. Marine insisted that with me at her side she wouldn't be scared of anything. I'd watch her face, with her waggling the joystick as she ducked and dived in and out of spaceships on the screen. I thought how one day my precious girl would have to navigate journeys without me, outside of the safety of this booth, and my heart ached. At vital moments in the game I grabbed the joystick or made a shot on her behalf, to keep her in it. But I couldn't help wondering how I could protect her when she took on the real world. In there we could take on the forces of evil, just the two of us, and win every time. But what would it be like out there, when the ride was turned off, and the bright lights had faded. When the cold wind of the outside world blasted onto Marine?

After the game, I held her hand and walked her to the car. She got inside it and strapped on her seatbelt. Like many children, Marine was far more intuitive than people credited.

'Are you okay, Daddy?' she asked.

I gripped the buckle of my seatbelt for a minute, and turned to her. 'I just want you to know something,' I said, to her.

'What is it?'

I watched the children leave the fair, clasping in their fists bright clouds of pink candyfloss. The teenagers on their bikes eyeing them as they moved.

'I - I want you to know that I love you.'

'I already know that,' she said.

'Yes. But I want you to know that whatever happens, I'm always on your side. Do you understand?'

She turned to me, and I wondered if her nose was about to wrinkle.

'I think so.'

'What I'm saying is, that you could do anything - anything at all, and -'

I couldn't find the words.

'You could even find yourself in loads of trouble.'

'Like what?'

'Like say you accidently killed someone. You could still come to me and I would always be on your side. No matter what.'

Marine considered this.

'Thanks. I would be on your side too.'

I waited until the children crossed the road.

'Thanks,' I said.

FOUR

EVERYTHING CHANGED on the 3rd October. We were holding a tea party. I took it as proof of how much confidence Juliette had gained, for her to suggest leaving Christian with a babysitter for the afternoon and hosting a party. To celebrate the success of Phillip's most recent tour.

After a successful run in Edinburgh, Phillip gained critical acclaim for his stand-up show. It was a performance which saw him variously adopt the persona of a corrupt MP (too minor to fully exploit his post), a colonialist (talking fondly of a country that didn't exist) and a zookeeper (in search of a zoo that we gradually learnt had no animals). The show veered between political satire and goofy physical comedy, and it had been strange to see his ever-lengthening quiff in more and more newspapers as time went on. Unfortunately, I wasn't able to mock Phillip for being the new darling of the press, because I knew he could easily say the same about me. People occasionally stopped me in the street and shouted phrases I'd used on the show. A bloke in a bakery asked me if I had kept my nurses' outfit. It was weird to have young, male students stop me in the street when I was out shopping, asking if I fancied a quick game of Halloween Booby Trap IV. When I mocked Phillip, for attending the opening of every envelope he was invited to, he responded by asking when my first appearance on 'I'm A Celebrity Get Me Out of Here' would be.

Our repartee didn't address the slightly scarier fact that Phillip was becoming even more famous. Juliette had insisted on us hosting the party when Phillip won a prestigious Aerial Award, said to be the British equivalent of an Oscar for comedy. Marine was on a school trip for the day so our house was filled with the aspiring actors, TV panelists and agents that Phillip had accumulated as his new coterie. To the assembled bodies, that sipped champagne in the living room, I gave a brief toast to Phillip. Asking everyone to raise their glasses for a man who 'has paved the way for those using humour to evade meaningful employment'. Phillip, in turn, raised a glass to 'a man who's used teaching to avoid becoming a functioning human being'.

When the laughter had died down, Christine drifted to Phillip's side as I approached them. 'Honestly,' she was saying. 'Ben and Juliette host a beautiful party for you, Phillip, and in return you say that your best friend is "barely functional".'

'Ironic really,' I said, throwing a peanut into my mouth. 'At university he always used to say I was *too* functional.'

'Every day, you used to sharpen your pencils before lectures,' he said. 'And I'm sure I saw you iron your socks at least once.'

'The hall of residence didn't even have an iron,' I said. 'So that proves what you know.'

'You're the only student that asked for one,' Phillip replied.

'I'm with Ben on this,' Christine said, patting Phillip's arm affectionately. 'Phillip still doesn't iron. Before big occasions I'm sure he forces me to do it by pretending he doesn't know how.'

'Impressive, isn't it?' he said, wrapping his arm around his girlfriend's neck. 'I get into a relationship with a strident feminist, and persuade her to do my shirts for me?'

She rolled her eyes, smiling. 'Oh yes. Very clever,' she said.

As the guests threw canapés down their throats, a squat man with fierce eyes cornered me by the breadsticks. 'Art Golightly,' he said, thrusting out a hand. 'Phillip's agent. You two have great chemistry.'

'It's not chemistry, its resentment,' I said.

He threw back his head and laughed. It was a singular honk, the abrupt beginning to a bagpipe tune. 'You see?' he said, drawing glances. 'That's what I mean. You're getting a lot of praise for that show of yours, what is it, Educating Croydon?'

'Bristol,' I said, imagining that my breadstick was a foil that I could ward him off with.

He nodded. His eyes darted around me, as if calculating the weight of the web required to capture me with. 'Did you know, you were "Pick of the Week" in the Radio Times yesterday?' he said. 'Not the show itself, but the famous Mr. Pendleton. Champion of the underdog. We should talk. I could make you a rich man in a very short space of time. Think about it, you teachers earn peanuts. Not even peanuts - monkey nuts. Come on, what do you say?'

His voice had taken on an American tinge. I looked behind him, as Phillip leant against a pillar. I noticed the collar of his dinner jacket was turned up, betraying that he'd been trying to act suave. He smiled rakishly at me, Christine hovering in the distance behind him.

'So, what do you say?' Art repeated.

I smiled. 'I say, that you need a proper drink,' I answered, taking his empty glass.

It was then that the phone rang.

For some reason, I glanced at the clock the moment it blazed to life. It was 3.05 p.m. I placed the glass carefully on a table and answered the call. I had not been prepared for the silence that greeted me as I picked up the handset. At first I wondered if it was a wrong number, but the voice on the end of the line that eventually spoke was panicked, almost hysterical. I struggled to make it out at first, given the cacophony of noise around me.

'Who is this?' I asked.

'Mr. Pendleton, it's about Marine.'

'What's happened?'

I tried to seal off the noise around me, and covered my free hand with my other ear.

'I'm afraid - I'm afraid she's taken a fall. A bad one.'

'A fall? Off what?'

'The school party was walking along the top of the moors and - Marine somehow fell behind the others. One of the assistants dropped back to see if she was okay, and I'm told Marine was found dangerously close to the cliff-edge.'

'Jesus.' I looked for my keys. 'Is she okay?'

The voice didn't answer straight away. 'I'm on the phone to him now,' she said, to someone else in her room. 'Mr. Pendleton, I understand she has taken quite a fall. The paramedics have been called out and - they are trying to find her.'

'Trying to find her? How far did she fall?'

'We don't know.' Her note of panic in her voice terrified me. 'I'm so sorry,' she said. 'We don't know,' she repeated.

'You don't know where she is?'

'They are locating her right now.'

'Locating her? What do you mean "locating her"?'

Phillip collected himself at my side, and leant in to the handset. It sounded as if someone was taking the phone from her.

Chastising her vaguely under his breath.

'Mr. Pendleton, Mark Reynolds. Can I ask that you and Juliette come into the school as a matter of urgency?'

I was grabbing my coat even as I hung up the phone.

Juliette appeared in the doorway, holding a dish. 'What is it? What's happened?'

'It's Marine. She's taken a fall.'

The blood drained from her face.

'Is she alright?'

'I don't know.'

The plate slid from Juliette's hands. In the second after it smashed on the floor, an image lodged in my mind that, in the days to come, I couldn't shake. Canapés stuck to her leg. Sliding down her calf as she stood there. Rooted to the spot.

We drove to the school. 'We've got to get straight to Marine,' Juliette said, as I drove the car into the first space.

'I'll get the address of this moor and we'll go,' I answered.

I made Juliette wait in the car. I ran into the school office.

As soon as I walked into the secretary's office I knew it was serious. The office had the strained air of a crime scene. The man and the two women clustered around the phone all looked pale. At least two of them were shaking.

'Mr. Pendleton, Mark Reynolds,' said the man, his bald head glistening as he seized my hand.

'Have they found her?'

'Mr. Walker has just phoned us again. He is the one who saw her fall.'

'Who's Mr. Walker?'

'Agency staff. He was helping Katy with the children today. He's given me an address. The paramedics are with Marine now.'

'Is she alive?'

He looked down, pushing his hands hard into his pockets. 'We don't know anything yet, I'm afraid she took a nasty fall.'

'You need to tell me what that means.' I heard the words echo in the room, and fade. I felt as if my soul had been hollowed out in one, ruthless cleave.

A thin woman burst in, clutching a rucksack. 'Mark, here it is,' she said, handing it to him. Mark grabbed the bag.

'My keys,' he said, looking frantically inside. 'Jesus Christ, you left the keys on my desk,' he said, bolting out of the room.

'Can I call this Mr. Walker?' I said, to the two secretaries standing mute nearby. 'It seems he was the last member of staff to see her.'

'Mr. Walker? Oh, God,' said the thin woman.

I took her in, the white-blonde hair and the glassy expression.

'What does that mean?' I said, stepping closer to her. 'Why "Mr Walker, oh God"?'

I looked over at the plump, red-faced secretary holding the phone. She shot a hostile look at the thin woman, who finally answered. 'Only because … we don't even have his number.'

'Lorraine,' said the plumper woman, 'let's keep a level head. This is not the time for gossip. Mr. Pendleton needs your help right now. Come on.'

Lorraine suppressed a grimace.

From outside, Colin barked the name Rose, and Lorraine's accuser ran to him. The natural authority of her heft was undermined by the clear tremor of her head as she departed.

'Why did you react like that when I asked about Mr. Walker?' I asked Lorraine. 'Who is this man?'

'He's agency. With the strike, he came in at the last minute.'

Rose appeared in the doorway. 'Lorraine, Mr. Reynolds' office. Now. Mr. Pendleton, Mark is ready to go.'

We trailed behind Mark in the car. Rain streaked the window as we drove out to the moor. Juliette remained silent all the way there. When we were stopped by lights, she exhaled loudly. Glancing over, I noticed her lips had lost their colour. As we drove out of the city, the grey surroundings merged into a wet green blur. I was almost glad of the sound of the passing rain. It was the only relief I got from the utter hatred I felt for every car in front of me.

We followed Mark's car into a car park, where a wet sign advertised 'The Tanners Moor Trail'. I drove the car into the nearest bay and yanked the keys from the ignition. We tore the doors open, and ran to the knot of people gathered in the car park. At the far end of it, I could see Marine's teacher Katy, talking to a coach driver. Behind its misted windows could just about make out the children inside. I tried to pick out Marine's face amongst them. When I couldn't, I told myself that it didn't mean anything.

We ran to where Katy pointed, a part of the hill evident only by a flickering piece of white tape. 'Why the hell is there tape?' Juliette asked. It hurt to consider reasons. Rain slashed at us as we clambered towards the white flicker. Juliette's party dress was wet through by the time we reached the crest of the hill. The slime from the canapés had mixed with mud on her leg. We hurried towards a group of people, a good fifty yards from the footpath where the grass had grown long, and the landscape was obscured by vegetation. Amongst them I recognized the uniforms of policeman and paramedics. I could see where the grass ended, into a presumably sharp fall. Police were lining the crest of the hill. To our horror everyone was looking down into the ravine. 'Where's Marine, where's Marine?' Juliette shouted. She addressed everyone in turn as we drew level, her voice growing shrill. 'Where is my daughter?' she screamed.

My heart pulsed so hard I was sure something inside would

break. I desperately hoped that when I peered over the edge I would see Marine on a ledge just under it. Sat there, with a scratched knee and a brave smile. A paramedic looking over her, with one hand on her shoulder. As I looked vainly over the edge I saw thick tangle of thorns, and through them a hundred foot drop, broken by the odd chalky ledge.

'Where is she?' I asked a police officer. He was clutching a walkie-talkie clasped to his fluorescent yellow jacket. His glasses were peppered with rain. Before he could answer a man in a green wax coat pushed in front of me.

'Detective Inspector Grayson,' he said, his nose wrinkling at the wind.

Behind him was a hunched man with a dirty grey hair, in an Arran sweater. He kept nodding for no reason at the policeman, stroking his chin, and then turning away from him.

'She's with the paramedics at the bottom,' Grayson said. 'Mr. Pendleton,' he said, waving at the man in the sweater. 'David Walker.'

Walker turned towards us as his name was used.

'Mr. Walker rushed back to fetch Marine after she fell behind,' the policeman said. 'He said she was looking for a -'

'No, looking for *some* flowers by the cliff edge. Yes, yes,' Walker said, as if agreeing with himself. The policeman turned his back to us as someone radioed him. Walker stepped forward. I got a whiff of carbolic soap and dried sweat. 'I ran back from the rest of the kids to get her clear,' he said, running a hand over his stubbly chin. 'I shouted at her to get back from the edge, but she just kept getting closer to it,' he continued. 'I slipped and fell–' he pointed at a long mark of mud on his left thigh, 'and when I got up I am sure I saw her fall off the edge.'

'Oh Jesus,' Juliette whispered, grabbing my arm.

'And she was wearing a red coat?' said the policeman.

Walker nodded.

'Her grandma bought her that,' Juliette said. I put my arm around her, and held her tight.

'We may have to have to isolate this area for the CSI's,' Grayson said, to the policeman. 'With this weather any evidence might well get swept away, but I want to preserve it as best we can. Is that understood?'

The policeman nodded, before leaning into a murmur from his walkie-talkie. 'They have Marine,' he said. 'The car park - let's go.'

Juliette ran ahead of me to the car park.

In all my life I had never known her to be so determined. She ran so hard, it was as if she was drawing from a source of strength that she had never revealed before. Her white party dress clung to her slim body as she ran into the rain, her heels abandoned somewhere into the mud. As I followed her I had a flashing memory of that time I lost sight of her in the sea.

The policeman ran, a few paces behind me. I was so frantic to get to the car park that I tripped twice, once catching my foot in a muddy pothole. Juliette ran stoically ahead of me, into the wind, and she never paused once.

In the car park the coach with Katy had gone. A blue-flashing ambulance had replaced it. As I ran the final steps to catch up with my Juliette, I saw a paramedic stand up, and open his arms to me. As I got closer I saw a small, orange carrier, with Marine strapped onto it. Her eyes were closed. Juliette started sobbing, and when a paramedic told her not to touch Marine her sobs grew louder. I knew then that hell existed, and I've never doubted it since.

We crouched down next to our daughter. My hand touched a bloody scar, lined with mud, on her little forehead. As I touched her skin, I called her my darling girl. Something plummeted in my heart as I realized she was cold. She looked just like she did on Sunday mornings, when we went into her room to wake her for a day of fun. Just as still, just as silent. 'Marine,' I said. Something seemed to break in my ribcage, and I knew I couldn't replace it.

'Is she in a coma?' Juliette said.

'I'm so sorry,' another paramedic said. 'We've lost her. We think she hit her head on the way down.'

Juliette wailed.

'She couldn't have suffered,' the paramedic said. 'She couldn't have suffered at all.'

AN HONEST DECEIT

PART TWO

FIVE

MARINE'S FUNERAL took place eight days later, on a bright autumn morning. Given the vague circumstances surrounding her death, Juliette and I had some difficult questions to answer about her post-mortem. Neither of us were able to fully process them in the way that we should have done.

That phone call at the party had instantly split Juliette and I back into separate entities, after all the work that had gone into our relationship. Juliette's grief carved out new space that I didn't trespass onto. Ever since the call I had stopped being a functioning member of the world. I didn't work, and I barely spoke, except to those few people in our lives that we have to relate to in such instances.

The night before the funeral I slept in Christian's room, and was awoken in the morning by a piercing bar of white light at the window. It was insane to think that I now had to bury my little Marine, and the thought rendered me immobile. I looked out of the window, onto a landscape covered with the wet papier-mâché of leaves. Soon, I knew, the wind would blow that temporary beauty away and the ugly grey swell of the world would reveal itself again. I didn't see why I had to deal with it any more. The world hadn't played by the rules, as far as I was concerned. I didn't see why I had to either.

Juliette was a ghost. Throughout the service she didn't speak, didn't cry, and was barely able to even look up at me. I wondered why she had decided not to invite her parents to the funeral. I knew that they were both very elderly, and I wondered if she was concerned at the thought of uprooting them from the south of France for the journey. I wondered too if perhaps she, for some reason, did not want them to see her in such distress. But somehow, the manner in which she dismissed any possibility of including them made me reject the idea.

I remember nothing of the funeral itself: except that it was one long black swell of agony. How could I comfort Juliette, when I knew that the nightmare wouldn't end? We had lost a force for positivity in our lives, which we would never replace. We had had so little time to enjoy her presence in our world. Consequently, I could only watch over these surreal events, too muted to even engage in mourning.

The funeral, though functional, was a cosmetic event. People traded useless grief commodities with one another, and intimacy dictated the market forces of their transactions. People arranged themselves in a hierarchy of sympathy so absolute, that some deemed it insensitive to even approach me. People looked at me and expected me to cry, and they looked at Juliette and wanted, despite themselves, to see signs that she had finally been unhinged by the world. We all know how life wounds us, and its scars fester and make us act towards one another in an unkind way which we cannot justify. Such is our pain, that there is a part of human nature that wants to see evidence that another person has been dealt a mortal blow. I could see, from the way that people looked at Juliette, that part of them hoped to go away and say, 'she's a broken woman'. I loathed any sign of that tendency.

Does it make me a bad father, because I was barely able to speak, let alone cry on that day? Is it wrong that I was consumed with merely creating an occasion fitting for my daughter? I desperately did not want to look back and regret failing to give Marine the event she deserved. But I went through that duty so bloodlessly, that I despised my own pragmatism. I wanted Juliette and I to look back on that day with sadness and pride, and I wanted her to be a part of my effort. We failed, and I lament that.

It was not what a funeral should be – a monument, an abstract articulation of the essence of a human's life. It was a hollow game, an empty pact, and I could not find Marine anywhere in the incense, the curtains, and the popular lamentations. My daughter had been vivacious, enigmatic, and charismatic. She deserved poetry, music, or at least some kind of artful representation that summed up the bright daubing she left on this world. I did not have the strength to ask God to usher me through the day, but I felt him standing over me, as mute as he was when she fell.

Everyone thinks that their daughter is special, that their children somehow have something to offer that is irreplaceable. The difference is that Marine actually did have something unique to give to the world. Our lives are, too often, mundane and repetitive. People frequently lack courage or imagination, and colour their existence only with the unconvincing ink of bitterness. But Marine had an essence that could have illuminated the world. She was an inspiration; you only had to look at the way she inspired Juliette to emerge from her shadows to see that. And yet we were forced to commemorate her passing with a sudden, sombre day of nothing.

I had assumed that in the wake of this disaster Juliette and I would merge into one organism, which drew nourishment from a hidden source. I'd assumed that the myriad details of our mourning would be mirrored in one another. That our one comfort would be that we would transcend any of the barriers that usually separate human beings. But what was so ludicrous, so painful, was that we did not unite. Life had taught us to smile at our peers, to endure our private miseries, and to secretly harbour our own ambitions. It had taught us to keep ourselves clean and presentable, and perhaps how to occasionally even be beautiful. It had taught us how to sometimes make money. But it had never given us the equipment by which to traverse the bounds of skin and flesh that force us to merely bump up against each other.

In the days after the funeral Juliette and I were wordless, because there now were no words now. Our house was a tomb, in which I felt sure there could be no light. Not when a reckless universe had played so wildly with our souls. The world, with all its petty bureaucracies, bruised us as much as it wanted to. Philip and Christine came to share in the silence, and to bite their lips with us. I noticed that whenever they tried to reach a consensus of sympathy in front of Juliette they completely lacked the language. Phillip dealt in dry, heartfelt statements of fact. He'd puncture the silence by saying 'It is a tragedy', or 'let me know if there is anything can do'. Christine attempted to embark on quasi-spiritual riffs. 'Why do these things have to happen?' she would whisper.

Regardless, people still needed paying. People's obsessions still had to be tended to, and the world kept turning. We occasionally gripped each other in tears, like scarecrows propped against one another in filthy rain. But mostly we stood in silence, hunched at some sink or other. I felt I could not cry, because I did not know how or why my daughter was gone.

The distant land that I had slowly coaxed Juliette from had become her home again. I needed comfort, but we were not at that time, able to offer that to one another. So, in lieu of comfort, I began to crave answers about what had really happened on the moor.

SIX

'MUM, WHERE do fish go in the winter? They're not in the sea any more, I've checked.'

It must have been close to four in the morning when I heard those words again. An hour which, I believe, no human should ever be awake for.

I was woken by Marine's words. Lilting, removed, as if uttered from a very different place. I wondered if I was dreaming. Juliette's scent on the sheets - lavender, with a hint of conditioner - told me that this was real.

Her side of the bed was empty - just a dismissed ruffle of sheets. Sitting up, I heard a shuffle in the living room. I stumped over to it, my bare feet twitching on the cold floor, on which every grain of dust was sharply felt.

Juliette was there, in the window. Sat in the dreadful half-light of morning. The sun, leering in through the open shaft of window, lit her face into a pale shade of ivory. She was wearing her white pyjamas and clasping Snugglepuss, Marine's favourite toy, to herself. I stood on the threshold to the room for a moment, and hardly dared to step into its glassy surface. Juliette, shrouded in that strange light, seemed to me then like some evocation of the Madonna. Sacred in her own grief.

'Mummy,' she was whispering, rocking into Snugglepuss. 'Mummy, mummy, mummy, mummy.'

She was meditating, now. I knew the rhythms of her speech only too well. I recognized in her voice the timbre of her daughter's, which she was trying to replicate.

It was only as I restrained myself from disturbing her, that I realized Marine was alive inside Juliette. That Juliette was mining inside herself, to grasp her daughter once again. It was agonizing to watch her tunnel so ruthlessly into her own flesh, for an essence that could only retreat with time. Soon, I knew, Marine would become formless and then we should shape her through some mental communion. I knew that even with Juliette's deep love, she could never master the discipline to reach for Marine's pure essence at will. It was gone.

But watching her rock, I also felt envious. At least Juliette had Marine somewhere within her. She possessed her in a way that I never could.

Every time Juliette repeated the word 'Mummy' she captured the questioning, intrigued lilt of her daughter's voice in a way my voice never could. Marine, was, in that ruined morning, there. She was in the fragile texture of the morning. Not yet fully formed. She embodied Juliette's inflections, flitting in and out, too abstract to grasp.

I stepped forward, and for a moment Juliette was enclosed in a beam of sunlight. She looked up, and I could see lines on her face, nuances of emotion that I had never seen before. 'Mummy,' she repeated, looking up at me. 'Mummy.' She was part of a landscape I would never reach.

Juliette was not looking at me, but past me. Yet, at the same time, she held out her hand. Somehow, in this liminal state, Juliette was trying to draw me into this ritual. So that we that we could shelter in it together.

I looked down on her, my eyes tracing her pastel lips, grey with grief. Finally, her eyes began to focus and they narrowed upon me. 'Where do fish go in the winter?' she whispered, crouching inside each word. Savouring each one. 'They're not in the sea any more. I've checked, Mum. I've checked.'

I stepped forward. Juliette looked up at me, hungrily. The parts of her soul that I could see looked famished. I passed my arms around her shoulders and Snugglepuss fell to the floor. Juliette grasped me harder than she had ever done before. She sobbed, searching my back for muscular strength. 'I love you,' she whispered, the end of the sentence lost as she began to cry. 'Please don't leave me.'

I held her, tight. I tried to squeeze the grief from her delicate body until my shoulders were wet with tears, and amongst the tears I heard the same word repeated. 'Mum, mum, mum.' Juliette repeated the word again and again, there in the window, as we moved the couch. Like animals sheltering from winter, we fell into one another's arms. We slept as if we had been awake for days, and as if we had finally remembered how to do it. We slept ravenously, as if we believed we would emerge in the morning cleansed. With Marine standing there, smiling and barefoot in our kitchen. Forced from that lunar landscape because we'd earned her through grief.

It felt delicious, just then, to dream of Marine. I saw no reason why I could not dare to dream for her return, and to dream that doing so might be enough.

SEVEN

IT WAS KRAVER who pulled me into his office.

In retrospect, I'd returned to work too quickly. But I saw no alternative. Juliette needed regularity, in order for us to crest this dark wave. I didn't want Christian to be pulled too far into our grief, and I thought it important we maintain a façade of normality. I saw no value in staying in the house in my dressing gown, lamenting.

I was midway through an English class, trying to describe continuous verbs to a class of Year 10s. Some students had heard about what had happened, and a couple had even softly offered condolences whilst leaving a class. This had made me determined to grit my teeth and continue teaching them. But during that lesson, through the window, I saw a young girl in a red jacket, and my heart almost stopped.

She was clasping her mother's hand at the school gate. They were looking to cross to go to the school opposite: Marine's school. I stopped mid-sentence, and waited for the girl to look sideways. Waiting, as the whole classed watched, for affirmation that this was not Marine.

'Sir?'

I looked up. The class were all staring at me. 'Sir?' a boy said, *sotto voce*. 'You were saying?'

It was then that the door opened. Kraver, in a red satin waistcoat, held open the door and said 'I'd like to see Mr. Pendleton in my office, right away if he would so please.'

His office was larger, and emptier, than I had imagined it would be. As I followed the direction of his hand, I noticed that he had also commandeered the office next door to his, usually reserved for the deputy headmaster. A young, blonde secretary was stationed there, sitting rigidly.

His wood-panelled office, lined with boxes, overlooked the empty playground. Lyrca cycling shorts seemed to be drying on the radiator, and he'd installed a small fridge in one corner. I noticed that the walls were bare, the pictures of his predecessors having been torn down.

'You quite ready for all this teaching malarkey?' He asked, skirting his desk. He pulled a cigar out of his top drawer, lit it, and nodded at me as he began puffing. He sat, and offered me the seat opposite with an impatient wave. I carefully accepted the invitation.

I looked past him, at the empty space in the playground where the girl in the red coat had been. 'I'm trying to do what I can to help the whole family move on,' I said.

'I see, I see,' he said, rocking into the smoke. 'And how is that going, thus far?'

I reprimanded myself. His eyes narrowed in a manner that somehow warned me not to be candid.

'I think Juliette and I can only begin to move on once we know how our daughter died.'

He raised his chin. 'But you know how she died, don't you?'

he said, motioning with the cigar. 'She ran to the edge to look at flowers, didn't she, and then she tripped. That's it. End of.'

'I just don't quite feel satisfied with that explanation,' I said, watching closely for his reaction. 'Marine just wouldn't do that.'

I was surprised at the instant change in the air, the sudden squeeze in the atmosphere. Kraver's shoulders grew in size. I wondered if an imperceptible shift had occurred in my life, just then. It felt like the start of something. I heard myself say, 'She was always so scared of getting lost, and she never had an interest in flowers. I just find it hard to believe that she would lag behind the others like that.'

He pursed his lips, prising something from between them with a finger. I imagined him then as a chess player, three moves ahead, consulting the board. Determined to make it look like he wasn't taking the game seriously, when you knew he was. 'It's perfectly natural,' he began, 'to be asking yourself questions. But isn't that what the school's enquiry is for? It decides what happened, once and for all.'

As he spoke, I noticed this curious movement in his hands. At the mention of an 'enquiry' his left hand spun into an upturned claw, and the fingers wriggled as he spoke. I could only relate the movement to that of a crab, flipped onto its back.

I adjusted myself in the chair. I realized there was nothing to lose. Not now.

'When I got the call about Marine, I came straight to the school. One of the secretaries - Lorraine, I think - reacted when a 'David Walker' was mentioned. Apparently he was the last to see her alive?'

'Reacted?' Kraver turned his head askew. 'How do you mean, reacted?'

The puffing seemed to intensify.

'Yes. When Lorraine was told that Mr. Walker had been with Marine, her exact reaction was "Oh God".'

He looked past me.

'Mr. Kraver?' I asked. He nodded. I couldn't read his eyes through the smoke. 'I hear he was agency staff, drafted in at the last minute?'

'I don't think you should pick on Katy. She was just doing her job. That would not be clever.'

The crab movement again. A strange, gestural scuttle. I wondered if it was a poker tell.

'I'm not questioning Katy about anything.'

'Well that's splendid.'

He stretched, and rocked on his chair. 'Bad things happen in life. That's the game we play. Some people deal with it, and others go looking for blame.'

'I don't want blame. I want an explanation of why this Lorraine–'

Kraver suddenly stood up. It was like a whip had been cracked. His mouth closed hard around the cigar. 'I came to see you today, Ben, to check if the shock of your daughter's death might affect you doing your job. But you're making life hard for me, by reacting this way. Very hard indeed.'

'I'm not sure what you mean?'

He raised his voice. 'I wanted to see if you were fit and ready to return to work. But clearly, there are questions to be asked about that.'

'Questions?' I leant forward. As I did I saw that his skin had a matted, grizzled tone to it that I had never noticed before. 'I merely wanted to check if–'

'The enquiry will check all these things, Ben.' He leaned forward, and his lips spread into a subtle smile. When he next spoke his voice was sonorous. It was rich enough to soak up any sense that his authority was being threatened. 'That's what they're for. Isn't it?' The smile widened. 'Eh?'

I realized he was speaking to me as if I was a child who'd dropped an ice-cream, and that he was telling me I could easily get another. For a moment I almost felt like that was the case. I gathered my thoughts.

'So the enquiry will question everyone at the scene that day? Walker, Katy, Lorraine?'

He looked out of the window.

'You've not been involved in an enquiry before, have you?' The rich voice returned. He opened his palms. 'I can tell,' he said, shaking his head, as if sympathetic to that. Kraver moved around the desk. He positioned himself so he was standing over me, hands on his hips. The smoke had mixed with an intense aftershave to create an unusual scent. 'Just let the enquiry take its course. In the fullness of time I am sure it will conclude that this was an unfortunate event ...'

'How do you know what it will conclude?' I asked.

'But in the meantime,' he said, stretching the vowels. 'I suggest - no I require - that you take some further time off. Time to recover. Don't trouble the other staff about this. You're a smart man. A man of the world, like me. A little shorter in the tooth perhaps, but we can't hold that against you, can we? Either way, you know what a delicate operation it is, running a school.'

'You're forcing me to take leave?'

He moved to the door.

'Your desk will be waiting for you when you return,' he said, with a curt nod.

'I'm more worried about my job. Can I have that in writing?'

'You have my word, and as a principled man that will be enough for you. Won't it?' He raised his chin as he spoke, his face moving too high for me to catch his eye. 'Good day to you, Mr. Pendleton,' he announced, opening the door.

He turned to his secretary as I passed. 'Marilyn,' he said, 'just give me a few minutes before my next appointment.'

'I'm sorry Mr. Kraver,' she said, 'but Mr. Turner is already on his way up.'

'Well, you've made a pig's ear of my diary this morning, haven't you?' he said to her.

I lingered on the stairway, just out of his sight, as she apologized profusely. I heard the leafing of pages. 'You're an embarrassment on days like this, really,' he was saying. 'You either do it my way, or it's the highway. Have I made that clear?' he boomed.

EIGHT

I RUSHED TO TELL Juliette about this development. I got straight into the car, hurrying so much that I left some work documents I needed behind. Every traffic light was another barrier preventing me from releasing the pulsing, tension in my temples. In that meeting, in my mind, I had been fighting for answers that both Juliette and I needed. But Kraver had not only avoided helping, he had been positively aggressive during his evasions.

I parked the car on our street, my eyes following a girl in a scarlet coat, skipping at the end of it as I walked. I burst open the front door, leapt up the steps and pushed into our home. Juliette was standing in the living room window, with a white blanket around her shoulders. I couldn't see what she was looking for, in the low light of the evening. As I caught my breath I wondered if she too was watching the little girl in the coat.

'There's going to be an enquiry,' I said, placing my keys on the glass table. 'Kraver told me today. I think there is more to all this than meets the eye.'

She paused, and I wondered if I heard a sniff. 'What do you mean?' she asked, quietly.

'The teaching assistant who was with Katy Fergus on the day was drafted in at the very last minute. When I was at the school his name was mentioned and one of the secretaries sounded very concerned to hear he was there.'

She turned to me. The ochre light from a streetlamp bathed half of her face.

'What is it that concerned her?'

'She didn't tell me, and Kraver wouldn't either.'

'Will the enquiry tell us?' she asked.

'We have to make sure it does, don't we?' I said.

She stayed impassive. I wondered if I saw her bite her bottom lip.

'For Marine,' I said.

There was a momentary gap, and then her shoulders surged forward with a loud sob.

'I'm sorry,' I said, rushing forward, putting my arms around her. 'I shouldn't have said that. I need to keep a clear mind.'

She shook her head, moving it more and more vigorously as she considered my words. 'You're telling me someone might have been trying to hurt her?'

'I'm going to get to the bottom of it. I know it's upsetting - it's not something I want to even consider, either.'

She lifted her head, and the light blasted onto her face as she looked up at me.

'You don't understand,' she said. 'You don't understand why it's not - why I can't even think that someone might have been trying to ...'

'Of course I understand,' I said.

She looked at me, and for a second her features seemed to be deciding on an expression. 'I never told you,' she said, grasping my hand.

'Told me what?'

'I thought you'd have figured it out.'

'Figured out what?'

The light intensified.

'I can't think about someone trying to hurt Marine. It is my worst nightmare. When I was a little girl ...'

'No,' I said, smoothing her hair.

She nodded.

'My father.'

I lifted her head. I held her gaze, my eyes interrogating her face, as she slowly began to nod. The strong link between our eyes grew even more intense. 'Oh, Juliette,' I said. 'I didn't - I sometimes wondered if something had happened to make you so ... reticent.'

She cocked her head and began to cry. The pain, seeping out of her, was so great it was bewildering. So that was why she hadn't wanted her parents nearby. I held her, inhaling her scent, trying to breathe life into her body. The news was strangely liberating, in a horrible way. I craved more explanations.

I tried to carve a path through these thoughts, but they were too thick. Juliette's shoulders hunched, and I felt her become impenetrable. 'I really believe you'll be able to get some closure if we know what happened to Marine,' I said.

Juliette was immobile, and the remark rang out in the room, hollow and stupid.

I felt a surge of relief when the doorbell burst into life.

I paced downstairs, surprised at the chill of the outside world. When I opened the door, Katy was standing there, pensive. From under a red beret, her white-blonde curls were swaying in the wind. She seemed too anxious to smile.

'I am so sorry for your loss, Mr. Pendleton,' she said.

'I was going to come looking for you, strangely enough,' I said, noticing her nose was red from the cold.

'Shall I come in?'

I glanced behind me, at the dank stairwell. 'It's not a good time for that. Let's go for a drink. Somewhere warm,' I said.

NINE

THE PUB WAS almost empty. I'd chosen one that I knew would be desultory at this hour, and it hadn't let me down. As Katy sipped her Bloody Mary I spoke fast. Quiz machines pulsed distant melodies as I told her of Lorraine's reaction, and Kraver's threat. I tried to read the expression on her face, grasping my warm Guinness as I spoke. It wasn't that she seemed to be restraining her reactions, but her impassive face offered the impression of someone accustomed to hiding their feelings.

Once I'd finished she leant forward. Looking at her hands, Katy seemed determined to choose the correct words. I noticed then how doll-like she was, this young teacher who seemed to be sharply aware that she was about to swim out of her depth. I wondered what private negotiations had driven her to seek me out.

'In that case, I'm so glad I called around tonight,' she said. 'I wonder why my conscience didn't force me to sooner.'

'What do you mean?'

'Walker's story to the police was not accurate at all. I tried to tell them on the hillside, but I'm not sure they took it in. You see, I was walking at the front of the procession, and Walker's job was to ensure there were no stragglers. It's impossible that Marine could have broken away, as at that point the pathway was narrow, lined with hedges on both sides. She would have had to pass him to fall out of the line.'

'What are you saying?'

'When I heard Walker tell the police that she broke away, I assumed he was just panicking. Having chewed it over, I wanted to come to you to set the record straight. But this talk of Lorraine's reaction has got me thinking.'

She curled a lock of hair over her ear, inhaling steadily.

'I wasn't very happy that someone the children didn't know was appointed to assist me on the field trip. Experienced teachers like Miss Granger were also free that day, so I had no idea why Kraver appointed someone new. Or ignored my request for a second assistant. I found this Walker bloke a little odd on the coach ride out to the moor. He kept encouraging the children to sing, and I remember wondering if he'd even been with children before. I remember saying, 'You don't need to worry about this and that, you just back me up when I ask you to do something'. He seemed so keen to agree to everything I said, I just assumed it was nerves. Inexperience.'

'Okay.'

'But then, on the field trip, I became quite irritated with him. Having given him the job of being at the back of the crocodile, I did a head count at one point and we were two girls short. I had to force the whole trail to a standstill and rush back to see what the hell was going on. Walker was showing Marine, and another girl, flowers in the hedgerows. I had to tell him to get them to rejoin the trail so we could keep going.'

'Jesus.' I put my head in my hands.

'Wait a minute,' she said. 'See what you think of this. Twenty minutes later I did another head count, and we were one down again. I rushed back to see who was missing, and it was Marine. I was panicking now, as at the front of the line I was making these girls wait, and I couldn't quite see them through the mist. I ran back to the back to see what was going on and Walker was quite far away from where the line ended. I said 'what on earth are you doing? You just need to keep the girls in the line.' He had this look on his face which was - it was like he was embarrassed. Deeply embarrassed. I asked him what was going on. He told me that Marine had broken away to look at flowers, and that she was dangerously near the cliff edge. I told him to go and get her while I got all the girls together in a group, where I could see them. I was panicking now. As quickly as possible I tramped closer to the cliff edge, wondering where the hell Marine had gone. Walker was shouting out for her. I heard a noise, a small scream and - in retrospect, I think that could have been the moment Marine fell.'

I shook my head, tried to bury the feeling in my gut.

'Why would Marine have refused to rejoin the procession?'

'This is just it. I'm starting to wonder if she ran when she saw Mr. Walker coming.'

I ran my hands through my hair.

'Oh my God,' I said. 'What do you mean?'

She took a long draught of her Bloody Mary. I noticed her Hello Kitty purse on the table, and the illuminated desktop on her mobile phone, next to it. It held a picture of a blonde burlesque dancer, swinging from a trapeze. I wondered if it was her. I've never considered her to be more than Marine's teacher, I thought. But she maintains a whole world behind the scenes that is kept hidden. Yet here she is, risking its exposure.

'What I'm saying is, I wonder if it was more than just incompetence which allowed Marine to get close to the cliff edge.'

Something in me snapped.

'Promise me something,' I said. 'Promise me that when Kraver calls on you to speak in the enquiry, you say all you said just now.'

'I'm thinking of emailing him tomorrow.'

The mildness of her language irritated me. Dealing with Kraver, I somehow knew that accuracy - complete precision - was required. It frustrated me to think that the sharpness of her intent would soon be blunted by my absence.

'You do that,' I said. I took a few heady, long slugs of Guinness. 'It's so important the school has this evidence for their investigation. And that the jury hear this when the legal investigation begins.'

'So what's the next move?' she asked.

'The next move is, I find Lorraine and get to the bottom of what she knows about this Walker. First thing tomorrow morning.'

'I'm worried that if you go storming in there Kraver will be aggressive towards you. He's clearly a man who puts his ambitions first. I'm told the reason Miss Gregor wasn't approved as a third member of staff was because he seconded her to the New Eden site. But we're understaffed as it is.'

'I don't have a choice about telling Kraver. If he wraps up the investigation quickly, without taking all this into account, it'll be hard to get to the truth.'

'What does Juliette think?' Katy asked, grasping her drink.

'Right now, she's barely present. She can't handle all this, and who can blame her? Finding out exactly what happened that day is the only way to get her back, I think.'

'The d-. The accident. It happened very recently. It's normal that she needs to mourn, isn't it? Just give her time.'

'I don't feel like we have time. Something irreparable has

happened to Juliette. She's given up. It's not just like I am fighting for the truth. It's like I am fighting to get her back, as well.'

+ + + + +

The following Monday, I waited on a bench in the car park outside the school reception. A light layer of frost seemed to have bubbled through the cracks of the city in the night. I stood up, fast, when a matronly woman with a set of keys arrived. 'Can I help you?' she asked, finding the keyhole.

'I'm here to talk to Lorraine.'

'Shouldn't be long. Come in. You'll catch your death.'

Once I was inside a woman who I remembered as Rose caught a glimpse of me through the frosted window of the reception as she parked her car. Having gathered her belongings she seemed to be making her way rather reluctantly to the door. The moment she had opened it I was on my feet.

'I was wondering if I can speak to Lorraine?' I asked her.

'Oh,' she said, flustered. 'There's been a bit of a carry on with her. Lorraine got a call on Friday. She's been seconded.'

'Where to?'

'The New Eden site. You know, that new campus?'

She kept nodding as I followed her into the open plan office, where the only sound was from the low buzz of computers, waiting to be reminded of their purpose. The scent of recent coffee, harsh and instant, laced the air. 'We were a bit surprised, to be honest, that she was relocated so suddenly,' she continued, throwing a file onto a desk. 'She was only just beginning to settle down here.'

I closed the door behind us. Rose, unzipping her jacket, seemed to be waiting for my inevitable question.

'Do you have her number?'

She bit her lip. 'No,' she said.

'But you've heard about my daughter's death, I take it?'

'Yes,' she said,' clasping her hands in front of her. She shook them for a moment. 'I'm sorry. It's the worst kind of loss. My son lost a daughter on a boating accident a few years ago. Him and his wife have only just stopped reeling.'

'In which case, you more than anyone will know how desperate we both are to find out what really happened.'

I could see the war going on in her mind, as her knuckles whitened. I decided to press my advantage, instinct telling me I might succeed.

'To make completely sure no other parent has to know what it is like to see their son or daughter harmed.'

She bowed her head, then moved to the kettle. 'I can offer you a drink. Much more than that might be asking too much, though.'

'Lorraine reacted when David Walker was mentioned on the day of the fall,' I started, firmly, 'as if there was something about him that she wouldn't have wanted me to know.'

Rose shot a look past me, as a figure darted in the hallway.

'I don't know what you mean,' she said, shaken.

I feared the figure was Kraver, and that this brief opportunity would be lost in seconds. I decided to play the only card I had. I hoped she wouldn't guess what a low number I had on it.

'I have spoken to staff at the school,' I said. 'They told me you have some information I'd want to know.'

Her eyes widened.

'Mr. Pendleton, I understand why you're here, but I don't think it's a good idea for us to get into all of this,' she said. 'I think you'd be best off at home with your family.'

'After Lorraine reacted like that, you told her to not indulge in gossip. Now please. As a woman who knows the pain of what we are going through. What can you tell me?'

Her gaze lowered.

'What gossip are you talking about?' I pressed.

'Come on. It's more than my job is worth,' she said.

'I've lost a daughter, and am in danger of losing my partner to the fallout as well. If it is just gossip, then I don't see the harm in me knowing.'

This seemed to catch her, and she fleetingly met my eye.

'Please.'

She closed her eyes. 'If I tell you, will you promise that you won't let it get back to me? I'm only telling you because - because of my son.'

'Of course. Now, please. Speak.'

Like a child forced to recite an apology she spoke listlessly.

'Well, David Walker has rather a nasty cloud hanging over him. A few people went sniffing into his past, and Lorraine heard, from a friend's husband who works in the prison service, that he had been imprisoned. Before he changed his name.'

'Imprisoned for what?'

She levelled her gaze onto me. 'Oh God,' she said. 'This is worse than it sounds. Please try to restrain yourself, because I am pretty sure this is just rumours.'

'Imprisoned for what?'

'For offences against young girls.'

'Jesus Christ. And Kraver let him work here?'

She didn't move.

'Did the agency know about his past?'

'I assume Walker successfully got CRB clearance under a new name. Or, perhaps what's most likely is that the rumours are just that.' This seemed to comfort her. 'Yes,' she said, nodding. 'That must be it.'

'But what if they're not rumours? Did Kraver know that Walker had changed his name? That he had a criminal history?'

'He was informed, yes. So I assume those concerns came to nothing, and that's why they employed him.'

I started pacing, a tingling energy coursing through my hands. 'What the hell is Kraver doing, employing someone like that?'

'I have no idea,' she said, drawing towards her seat. 'I had to stamp the approval of a new employee, so I know he okayed it.'

'You agreed Walker's appointment, knowing these rumours?'

'Oh, Lord, I suppose I did, yes. But only after Kraver promised me that it had been looked into. I thought it best to move on. My husband had an injury at work recently, and we need to pay the bills. You must understand that?'

'You know there's going to be an enquiry? That all involved will be interviewed?'

'An enquiry?' she said, her mouth forming a small oval.

'A school enquiry, and in due course a legal enquiry. I don't think it's a case of 'moving on'. It's all bound to come out in the open.'

Her face grew pale. She cleared her throat. 'Yes,' she said. 'It looks like it is.'

TEN

A LETTER TOLD ME that in two months the school's enquiry would complete. The cool, impassive phrasing insisted that it would be a 'thorough' investigation. But it mentioned absolutely no specifics, and I wondered if Rose had sought out Kraver the minute I left the school. I still wasn't sure if she was more worried about her job than about getting justice for Marine. But what if I was wrong, and I was risking her livelihood for nothing?

I told Juliette that the enquiry would take place, as she slept softly that evening. Something made me reluctant to wake the immobile crescent at my side. Looking over the silver sheen that tinted our room, I wondered when our life had become so spectral.

The next day I had to retrieve some possessions from the school, and I saw a twitch at Kraver's curtain as I got into my car. The following day I got another letter from him, telling me I could no longer teach at the school. It said that this judgement had been made on the grounds of a decision by the school board that 'I was not ready to return to work, following a bereavement'. I wondered why he hadn't bothered to come downstairs and tell me to my face.

The looseness of his language, and the vague allusion to my own consent, rattled me.

Blood pulsed in my temples. I immediately phoned the school to contest the decision. The school told me that all I could do was write to their regulatory body, and wait for a response from them. I asked how long this would be, and the administrator, irritated, said, 'How long is a piece of string?'

Whilst I calculated the length of this string my life was in limbo. I knew two important investigations were also taking place - the school's enquiry and the legal enquiry, which I was assured would 'run in parallel with one another'.

I hated being a loose end, and I missed the frenzied rush of getting through a day of school. I decided to use the time to make sure the courts got all the information that needed consideration. But the policeman I spoke to, a PC Pollard, was so often away from his desk that I was grateful to even hear back from him. When I told him about Lorraine, Rose and Katy's concerns he interrupted me, saying "Yes, yes'. He promised that, 'The police investigation would look into all this'. But something told me he had long ago decided what the police would and would not look at. It was a horrible feeling, having someone in authority pay lip service to fair treatment when their behaviour showed that they had no shame about doing the opposite. But I told myself to trust in the processes. Perhaps this is just how investigations work, I thought. Kraver had picked up on my naivety about them.

It was darkest January when the letter from the school's enquiry arrived. I had hoped it would come before Christmas, as initially promised, but I was eventually told by the administrative office that it would be delayed until after the break.

All this made for a sedate, tense Christmas. Our first without Marine. Without the hubbub of opening stockings at a criminally early hour, with Juliette instead fixed to the window. I was at Phillip's house when I got the call, to say that Juliette had come home to a letter about their decision.

Phillip had just returned from a stand-up tour of America, and had texted to ask if I wanted to see a DVD of his final show. I had been glad to get out of the aching tension of our home. It had felt almost like an act of defiance to go to Phillip's cool, white, luxury flat. It overlooked a leafy park in which harried-looking people practiced yoga, and men with beards drummed alone, in a solitary paean to their own individuality.

At the door Phillip had greeted me with a lively punch on the arm. I noticed he was wearing a navy designer jumper Christine had bought him early in their relationship. He had now bored holes through the sleeves, through which he pushed his thumbs. I wondered briefly what she'd have thought of the modification. As he welcomed me in, his stubbly, strong features and bright eyes lifted my spirit.

His flat was a bit of a mess. The crescent of cream sofas in the lounge area strewn with empty wine bottles. The light from the park seemed to enter the room with some reluctance.

'Benjamin,' he said. 'I'm not even going to ask if you want a beer. With what's been going on I might as well throw the whole bloody crate at you right now. Am I right?'

'Where's Christine?' I said. 'I can't see her sanctioning alcohol intake during the day.'

Phillip brought me a beer from the fridge, the opened top oozing vapour as he passed it to me. The bathroom door opened, and a moment later a woman stepped softly into the doorway. As she looked up her eyes had a blend of softness and inquisition that I had never seen before. She rubbed her long blonde hair with a towel as she smiled at me.

'Heya,' she said, her voice tinged with a Durham accent.

It was only as she rounded the sofas, to sit next to Phillip, that I realized what a vision she was. Her supple flesh somehow shone, and she walked as if she was just becoming aware of the power of her body. She gently placed her slender feet on the glass coffee table, revealing, long, slender legs that stretched from her cotton summer dress.

'You sure I can't get you some grapefruit juice?' Phillip said to her. 'There's a cup of Earl Grey cooling in the kitchen.'

'I'm all right,' she said.

'Ben, this is Violet Isaken. We met at a talk the other day, about how social media exposes corruption. I was trying to research this character I'm working on but I didn't understand much of it. But Violet was there to explain it all to me, weren't you?'

'Yes. And I didn't speak down to him even once,' she said.

'Are you also a stand-up comedian?' I asked, already guessing the answer.

She shook her head, with a sweet smile. 'Only in my mind. Nah, I'm doing a Masters. About how the CIA tried to work out what made world leaders tick. They built up psychological profiles about each of them, so they could try to work out how to undermine them - if they needed to.'

'Sounds interesting,' I ventured. 'What have you found out so far?'

She reached for one of Christine's magazines. 'I don't know.' She looked at Phillip. 'That everyone seems to have a weakness that could potentially topple them?' As she followed the flickering pages I noticed that the tips of her hair, grazing her exposed shoulders, were almost white.

'Like what?'

She dropped the magazine and fluttered her eyelashes,

embarrassed by the attention. 'Like, I don't know, Castro's weakness was his ego. The world might have been very different if people had learnt to play on the weaknesses of men, you know,' she said, looking between Phillip and I.

'Violet's just had a paper published about some lost pages of a Hitler dossier that she discovered,' Phillip said.

It was strange to see him being obsequious. He hasn't won her over yet, I thought. But she must know that's what he's trying to do.

Violet nodded. 'Yeah. I found them by accident about three months into my study,' she said. 'My supervisor told me not to share the pages just yet. But I think he was just afraid I'd get more famous than him.' She pointed at herself as she said 'I', relishing the vowel.

'You've heard the saying, 'never outshine the master"?' Phillip asked.

'No, not until I met you,' she sang back. She looked at me. 'In the end I wrote off to a journal about it and then didn't I just become an overnight success?' She seemed to enjoy her sarcasm.

'Ben is a YouTube sensation,' Phillip said. 'He had an emotional meltdown in front of a teenager because she mentioned missing her mum. They're about to make hotdogs with his face on, or something.'

'Oh my God!' she exclaimed, snapping her feet onto the floor. 'I knew I recognized you!'

'Yeah, "Educating Bristol",' I said. 'That's what I do, 24/7.'

My bizarre use of an Americanism embarrassed me. But Violet seemed excited, leaning closer. I caught the scent of cocoa butter.

'I saw that episode where you got that girl to complete her exams and prove herself to her mam. I had tears in my eyes. I'm a fan.'

'I'm trying to convince him to sign to my agent,' Phillip said. 'But he doesn't trust suits.'

'Do it,' she said. 'Milk it for whatever you can.' She stood up. 'I should probably stop wasting your time and get my stuff together,' she said. 'Ben, been mint meeting you. Phillip, thanks for letting me use the shower. I couldn't have got a run in before my lecture otherwise.'

When she had left, I met Phillip's eye. 'What?' he said, with a slight smile.

'I have three words for you, and I know you know what they are.'

'What the–?'

'No, not those three words. Where is Christine?'

'We had an argument during the last tour. She thought I was partying too much, demanded I cut it short and come back home. I refused. She walked.'

'So you finished with her for a politics student, Phil? Really?'

'Violet hasn't replaced Christine. We got talking and we decided to stay in touch. We just got on.' Philip sat back.

'How well?'

'Well, I haven't got her to stay the night yet. She told you, she just used the shower.'

'Seems pretty strange.'

'Hers is on the blink. What could possibly be strange about that?"

'You being at a talk, for a start.'

'I'm taking my job seriously.'

'Trying to pull earnest young women, more like.'

'Come on, Ben. You know what your great flaw is? You know what the "biggest flaw in Ben" is?'

'From a man who's left his girlfriend on a point of principle?'

He smiled.

'Sure,' I said, indulging him. 'Go on.'

'Your love for Juliette is way too unconditional. Don't get me wrong, she's a great woman. But you've committed yourself to her so absolutely, you've given yourself no leverage!'

'Yeah, well, I remember what it was like being alone,' I said. 'I don't think you really know what it's like to have no options.'

'If you're a bit envious about me and Violet, Ben, that's totally normal.'

'There isn't a "Violet and you" yet, though is there?'

'Oh, I see. So I've got competition on my hands?'

'She's a young woman, Phillip. We're in our forties. That would be … pervy.'

He slapped his knee. 'That's where you're wrong, you recovering eunuch,' he said. 'The people Violet normally dates are kids. They don't have flats, cars, conditioner.'

I tried to raise an eyebrow, with mixed success.

'Smart women like that love a man with a few rings in his trunk.'

'I really don't know what you're on about,' I said. 'I've got far too much to lose.'

'So you're loyal to Juliette out of a fear of loneliness? Fear keeping you in line?'

'Not at all. It's just, you have to commit fully. Any half-measures and it won't work.'

'So how is Juliette at the moment? Any better?'

'No.' I sipped the beer. 'Not good.'

I told him about the enquiry. As I unravelled the whole story of Kraver, Rose, and Lorraine, I found myself squeezing an empty beer bottle he'd left on the table. When my recital ended I realized I was squeezing it so tight that I was surprised it hadn't shattered in my hands.

Listening to the story, Phillip conducted a strange dance around the room, tidying it as if preparing for some sort of onslaught that he knew was coming.

His phone, half-buried in the cushions next to me, blazed to life. Philip retrieved it, pushed its button, and pinned it against his shoulder. 'Hi, Juliette,' he said. 'We were just talking about you. Weren't we, Ben? Are you okay?' He nodded, briefly, then turned to me. 'She needs to speak to you, mate.' As he passed the phone he whispered, 'It sounds important.'

'Juliette?'

'It's the school's enquiry,' she said, her voice torn with anger. 'It's a total whitewash, Ben. They've not even sent us the report.'

'Oh, no?'

'It's just a summary letter saying "The school's procedures were in no way to blame for what was simply an accident". I'm going to get on the phone, and make sure the courts are considering everything we know before they come to a decision. The jury will be giving their verdict any day now, but if the police just go by what the school concluded then that enquiry is going to be a complete travesty too.'

'Jesus Christ,' I said, looking up at Phillip.

'I know,' Juliette replied. 'If the courts don't find anyone guilty either, I don't know what I'm going to do.'

+ + + + +

**SCHOOL TRIP DEATH 'NEEDS PROPER INVESTIGATION',
SAY PARENTS**
The parents of a schoolgirl, who fell to her death during a trek on a school trip, tonight launched a bitter attack against her school. They were commenting after a jury yesterday returned a verdict

of 'accidental death' on Marine Pendleton, 10, who fell whilst taking part in a school walk on Tanners Moor on 4th November.

In a statement the parents Juliette and Benjamin Pendleton said: 'We wish to express our profound disappointment at today's verdict.

'Our cherished daughter went away excited at the prospect of a fun day out with her school friends. Instead she was to never return. Marine was separated from her other schoolmates and she fell from the cliff, due to a lack of proper supervision.

'She should not have been allowed near the edge in the first place, and we are not satisfied that she would have done so if she had been professionally supervised.'

They said the tragedy, which was witnessed by a member of staff, could have been avoided if the school had fully assessed the risks.

'The school have had the opportunity to properly investigate how this could have happened, and whether more than two staff should have been assigned for over thirty children. They have chosen instead to whitewash over the whole affair. We are not convinced that all the staff on the school trip fulfilled their Duty Of Care towards Marine. We were surprised that the coroner did not ask more witnesses to answer questions from the jury,' they added.

The local education authority said it would not be holding an enquiry into the death. A spokesman for the County Council said it was gathering information but was 'perfectly happy' the school had followed all procedures. A police investigation was opened and an inquest later closed when it was reported to the coroner that no one was criminally responsible.

The jury of three men and seven women, at Cormley Magistrates Court, heard four days of evidence, including eyewitness accounts from the teachers caught up in the tragedy.

At one point, the jury broke off from its deliberations to ask why David Walker, a Teaching Assistant who had not previously worked with the pupils, was recruited for the trip. Walker was asked if he could have done more to prevent Marine falling over the cliff edge, given that he first reported her 'breaking away' from the group.

Coroner Gillian Wetherton concluded her summing up this morning, by telling the jury she would only accept a verdict of accidental death.

Wetherton said, 'I have evaluated the evidence submitted from the various investigations and they are not sufficient to fulfil criteria for an alternative verdict. This is not about determining criminal or civil responsibility. It is a fact-finding mission.

'However, I am going to make suggestions to certain bodies, including the education authority and Health and Safety Executive, drawing their attention to certain matters where I believe they should look at procedures and what has occurred here.'

She said it was, 'Not a case where those involved were indifferent to the obvious risk or had showed a high degree of negligence. Emotions need to be put on one side. I know that by issuing this verdict I may be disappointing the family, but I have no other choice.'

ELEVEN

THAT MONDAY it felt wrong going to the school to do something other than teach. As I drove through the gates, I saw that my usual parking space had already been filled. Kraver had clearly decided that I was going to be on permanent leave, and that was the end of the matter.

His receptionist stood up and then sat down very quickly when I arrived on the floor. I pointed at Kraver's door. 'Is he in?' I asked.

She flashed a finger against her lips. 'You'll have to wait, Mr. Pendleton. Please.'

I waited for two hours, increasingly conscious of the hushed, conspiratorial calls she was having with Kraver on the phone, that were just too quiet for me to hear. Clearly, he was checking to see if I was still waiting. But I was determined not to take out my irritation on the receptionist, who'd thereby serve again as a useful scapegoat for him.

'Can I just see him for a minute?' I asked her.

'He says he doesn't have a spare second,' she answered, her face betraying a little more.

In the end, the rising nausea was too bitter for me to handle. I stood up. 'I must demand that he spares me at least a minute of his time,' I said. 'He's decided I'm not able to teach, and has sent me a letter informing me of that rather than saying a single word to me in person,' I said.

'Mr. Pendleton, you can't go in there ...' she began.

I tore the door open. Kraver was smoking a cigar by the window.

'You don't look surprised to see me,' I said.

'Nothing surprises me,' he said, brightly.

'We received your letter on Friday, and I am just coming to let you know that we are not prepared to let the matter settle.'

'Well, that really is the wrong move,' he said, sitting down and weaving his fingers together.

He suspended the cigar in an ashtray on his desk. 'Let me tell you a little about how this place works. We get resources, you see,' he said, collecting an imaginary box with one hand and moving it to the other side of the table, 'and we use those resources to do certain things. No resources, no doing. We don't have the resources to keep conducting the kind of expensive enquiries you want.'

'You did not have a full enquiry, as you well know. It is a toothless exercise in formality, a whitewash.'

He closed his eyes. I pushed on.

'Lorraine Hannerty, and Katy Fergus, have both expressed concern to me about David Walker, who I understand has a history of interfering with young girls. A criminal record, no less - which you overlooked by employing him.'

Kraver stood up. It was sudden snap of movement which reminded me of a slack puppet being pulled taut. 'Oh no,' he roared, raising a fist. 'I will not start listening to unsubstantiated rumours in my office. Won't have it. No, no, no.'

'They remain unsubstantiated,' I said, raising my wavering

voice, 'because your enquiry did not even interview Katy Fergus, as you promised it would.'

He pulled his head to one side. Ash tipped from the cigar, and smouldered in the tray.

'And as for Lorraine Hannerty,' I continued, 'you knew that she had raised concerns about Walker, so you had her moved from this school to get her far away from this scandal.'

The word 'scandal', for some reason, made him smile, revealing a gold incisor.

He shook his head, in a small spasm that loosened his hair. 'Miss Hannerty?' he started. 'Who's talking about Miss Hannerty? I'm not. It's not the school's responsibility to question everyone and everything. It's our responsibility to teach, do you understand?'

'So you don't think Katy Fergus should have had her views on record? She led the trip!'

'Mr. Pendleton,' he said, waving a piece of paper. 'I hold here in my very hand, permission from our statutory body to undertake an investigation, following your request. We did just that. The enquiry decided who to interview for it, who best to speak to, and then interviewed them. Bish bash bosh, job done.'

'They were people who *you* deemed fit for the enquiry! It wasn't even an independent enquiry. You've inspected yourself. I can even tell it's your choice of phrasing in the summary letter. You do know that we weren't even given the whole report?'

He closed his eyes as he completed his statement. 'This file is now closed Mr Pendleton. But I will add one thing, for you now. I think it is a great shame that you want to use the scant resources we have left to try and root around in the dirt even more.'

'As my employer, you have a responsibility to record any of my concerns officially. I formally ask that you record today that I am unhappy with the validity of this report. That you recognise I will be pursuing it.'

'But you don't want to complain,' he said, flicking a sheaf of paper on his desk.

'Yes, I do.'

His voice grew rich. 'No, you don't. Because by so doing you will quite literally be taking facilities from the children's hands.' He mimed the grab with energetic hands. 'Like snatching milk from a baby.'

'You and I both know that the report is funded by the statutory body, not the school.'

This amused him. 'When have you run a school? Do you know what it entails? What you don't seem to understand,' he said, his voice dropping, 'is that to have an enquiry, you need people to take *part* in the enquiry. But who would have to take the time to take part in it now? We've got an Ofsted inspection coming up, parents' evenings, sports days. We're hard pressed enough as it is, and the Eden site needs help round the clock too. No, no, no. Lots to learn here. The legal enquiry is set to report soon. You want to wait and see what they say.'

'No, I don't. Because I suspect that if you have had anything to do with that report, it'll be a whitewash too. I get the distinct impression from what you've just said that you've drawn the police away from the school.'

'If you look on the report, it gives you the people you can respond to,' he said, his voice smooth. He placed the cigar back in his mouth, satisfied.

'My complaint would go straight back to you. All you have done today is confirm that you tampered with the report to cover you and Walker.'

'Hmm. And all you've done this morning, Mr. Pendleton, by

bursting in here making such outrageous claims, is to make me wonder whether or not you should be a teacher at all.'

'What?'

'You're making it hard for me,' he said, closing his eyes, and blowing out smoke. 'It's very difficult for a headmaster, when a young teacher like yourself, barely out of training college, wet behind the ears, comes storming in here and making such demands. How am I going to be able to give you a good report at your next appraisal? The kind of report that'll allow you to carry on at the school?'

'I've never had any complaints from the pupils. Only praise, so far.'

'Yes, but they haven't had to deal with you as you've been this morning, have they? Do you deny that this behaviour is unreasonable, aggressive? Giving me no choice but to suspend you more permanently?'

'Not at all – I–'

'The truth is, even before this enquiry there were doubts about you, you know.' He looked out of the window, toying with the cigar. 'Oh, yes,' he said, 'I heard some rumours. Worrying stuff. Very worrying indeed.'

'What rumours?'

'That your behaviour in this school, has at times gone far beyond the eccentric, and strayed into practices that we would have to see as … unfit.'

'What behaviour? You let a film crew into the school to show off its attributes and I was featured prominently.'

'Well yes, we had to make an entertaining package. But if you're going to go giving out videotapes of your TV appearances in place of a CV..' He laughed. 'Well, good luck wi' that.'

'But in my last assessment I was given a mark of "outstanding".'

Kraver winced. I wondered if he had considered this verbal rally in advance. Playing it out as he paced around his spacious, wood-panelled office, smoking and overlooking the foundations of his new empire.

'I've seen your file. It made for very interesting reading. That mark was for the standard of your delivery in class. But your marking came up a bit short, didn't it?'

'It was just one point for me to develop ...'

'Exactly. You're developing. That's it. You've got it. I also have you on record you telling Mr Smythe that you have sometimes not had the time to take breaks at work?'

'That is normal for any teacher. Are you saying you are never rushed off your feet?'

'Oooh,' he said, shaking the cigar. 'This confrontational attitude is not doing you any favours when I am trying to help you, is it? If you are asking if I am busy every minute of the day then naturally, yes, of course. But any teacher worth his salt knows when to take breaks. I'm sure you don't want to officially tell me that you didn't know that?'

'What exactly are you accusing me of?'

'Well, it is my duty to inform you that the wheels are in motion for us to now start to evaluate your Fitness to Practice.

'Fitness to Practice?'

'I'll be giving the National School for Teaching and Leadership a ring, to tell them of your behaviour this morning. Some people at the top will need to know about this. The office of the Secretary of State will be the ones to confirm that this matter needs a closer look and we will then organise a hearing.'

'I don't believe this.'

He carried on reciting, eyes closed.

'It'll be an informal Fitness to Practice hearing. You can fight against me about it now, if you want, of course. But it would be far better for you to engage with the process. I'm sure you can see that.'

'This isn't happening,' I said. 'I can't believe that I have to prepare for a farcical hearing, when I have just lost my daughter. I was the one to raise a concern about the school's role in that.'

'And as a result of your loss I think you are, at present, not fit to teach.'

'So I will now be on leave until the hearing?'

'You can call it that. But from the moment you receive the letter about the hearing in the post you're suspended anyway.'

'Suspended?'

He started smiling.

I understood then that I had been stupid enough to exactly follow the script he had planned for this conversation. I had been angry when he wanted me to be, and I had been shocked when he wanted me to be. Psychologically, Kraver had proven that it was not worth me trying to overcome him. With every attempt I sustained further damage. Until he had taken me to the point where I was almost obliterated from the game. In this game of chess, Kraver seemed to be staying a few clear steps in front of me. Having been raised to expect the mechanics of justice to whir into motion when required, this turn of events taught me something. Those mechanisms do not exist to allow fairness; they exist only so the powerful can engage with them, when they so wish.

Kraver smiled. 'Now I know this is hard. But let me stress that this suspension is just a formality when issues of Fitness to Practice are being examined. It isn't personal.'

'It feels pretty punitive to me,' I said.

'If I were you, I'd be a smart lad and not share what I have told you today with your former colleagues,' he said. 'In fact, I will be making a formal note that I have requested that, so if you do prattle about this to them the panel won't look kindly on it. You'll know more about the enquiry soon,' he said.

I pushed my hand through my hair. The situation had got worse since I had come in, not better. I had to go away and plan a strategy, I decided. So it was me writing the script now, not him.

Kraver's smile remained fixed. He had me on the ropes. Exposed, surprised. Open to a pummelling as vicious as he wanted it to be. Which, for some reason, he wanted to be very vicious indeed.

I found myself unable to go home straight away. As I walked out into the car park, several schoolchildren cheered in my direction. As I drew close to my car a boy from Year Ten, with thick-rimmed glasses, asked me when I would be coming back. I found myself numbly saying, 'As soon as possible, Colin'. Two Year Elevens told me they 'miss your classes, sir'. Somehow, I couldn't bring myself to tell them the truth about the situation. I wanted to protect them from the confusion of this life, if only for a few moments longer.

I phoned Juliette in the car, and gave her a blow-by-blow account of the meeting. Every time I paused for breath, all she said was 'Oh my God'. When I stopped speaking, I felt a nudge of disappointment as I waited for her elaborate response. 'What do you think?' I asked, putting the phone on speaker on the dashboard as I started to drive.

'I'm flabbergasted. Regardless of the fact that Kraver's turning the tables, did he need to suspend you? Do the regulations even allow him to do that in these instances?'

'I don't know.'

'We'll have to check it out. I just don't know what you want me to say to you right now, Ben.'

'What do you mean?'

'I don't know if you should have gone in there, guns blazing. I just think you might have pushed him to the point where he felt he had no choice but to get rid of you.'

'What?'

'I got in touch with the school regulatory body this morning, to tell them that we would be formally contesting the outcome of their investigation into Marine. When I eventually got to speak to someone who knew what they were on about, they confirmed that Kraver *had* decided which staff members to interview for the investigation.'

'So it was an internal investigation. Not independent at all.'

'That's right, it was completely biased. But I noticed that, having checked with a superior, the person I was talking to started to get a little sharp. She advised that I should be careful of going on record to contest the statutory body's choice to let the school conduct its own investigation. She said that at the end of the day, as the teachers' association, they would decide on your fitness.'

'Which suggests Kraver had already told them I'd have a case to answer?'

'Yes. But with this confrontation this morning, he might have been pushed to try and get rid of you all together, Ben.'

A burst of rain hit the window, and I found myself gridlocked. The bumper of my car pushed up against one in front. A tattered 'Keep Your Distance' sticker flapped in the wind. As I eased the window down, rain lashed onto my cheek.

'But what else could I have done?' I asked.

'I don't know. Maybe we should have waited a bit longer, for the legal enquiry to conclude, before going for Kraver. I'm worried that he's going to influence the outcome of the legal enquiry.'

'I think he already has!'

'But before today he might have still been weighing up whether to look at your Fitness to Practice. Now, you've given him a proper reason to.'

'Don't be ridiculous. He's planned all this.'

A lorry roared by, kicking dirty water against my window. A few drops clung to my hair, one finding my hand and running down a groove in my knuckle. It was at that moment that I felt a hot mist curl in my mind.

'Jesus, Ben,' she snapped. 'You can say all you want, but we're going to be pretty desperate for money in a month or two if this doesn't all blow over, fast.'

'What do you mean, "doesn't blow over"? Of course it won't have blown over. Kraver is trying to destroy my reputation. It's the only way to stop my criticisms hurting him!'

For a moment the line fuzzed.

'The most important thing is that we can keep paying the bills,' Juliette was saying. 'But how can we do that now you're suspended? It's bound to be *at least* eight weeks until the hearing, and he'll want to stretch it out as long as they can. To weaken your resources.'

'You'll just have to take the strain for a few months, Juliette. We'll stick together. We'll fight this thing.'

'Oh, Jesus.'

The phone crackled. 'What is it?' I asked.

'They told us today that the project I was supposed to be assigned to has fallen through. They're trying to put a bid together to salvage it but it'll be a few months until it gets off the ground, if at all. I was going to talk to you, and say that *you'll* have to take the strain for a bit.'

'What?'

'Don't you get it, Ben?' she hissed, her voice rising. 'You blowing your top with Kraver might just have ruined us!'

'Juliette,' I shouted. 'I am fighting for my livelihood here, for you and me, as well as Marine. What the hell else did you expect me to do, after all we've heard about Walker? Just let it lie? Leave him free to hurt someone else's daughter?'

I wasn't sure, but I thought I heard her use my name, before she hung up.

TWELVE

THE NEXT DAY all I could do was walk around the city, in a state of numbness. My feet pulsed into the ground, my agitation lost in useless steps which led to no resolution.

I can remember returning to our house, and being struck by how our once-vibrant home had changed. A low hum was throbbing through it, and I couldn't locate where the sound was coming from. We live in a world of many alarms, none of which sound our true concerns. Everything in the house - the tick of the grandfather clock, the pace of Juliette's movements - had slowed to a funereal pace. As I put my keys on the glass table, the noise so loud that I wondered if I had cracked the surface.

A letter on the doormat confirmed that the Fitness to Practice hearing would be in two and a half weeks' time. It said that I would be issued with something called an 'Interim Prohibition Order', banning me from teaching until the enquiry had concluded. It did not detail why I was having my fitness scrutinised all of a sudden. The only reference to any charges against me was one line towards the end. 'At the hearing we will be discussing the appropriateness of your behaviour on campus', it said.

Juliette appeared in the doorway to the kitchen, holding Christian's hand. She was dressed in a scarlet cardigan, one which I remembered her wearing when we first took Marine for dinner at a restaurant. At the end of the meal Marine had slept in its thick folds, Juliette tenderly kissing her head as her daughter fell still. I shook my head angrily, trying to dispel the searing pain that accompanied the memory. Juliette saw my reaction and took a step back.

'What is it?' I asked.

She let go of Christian, and looked at the floor.

'I'm waiting for your apology,' she whispered.

The thought of Marine's light snore, coupled with the sudden recollection of Kraver's incessant smile, forced a flare of anger through my insides. It ignited in my mouth.

'You want me to apologise?' I roared. 'I've been trying to get us some justice!'

Juliette nodded, her eyes tracing the shape of the panels on the floor in saccadic movements. Christian began to cry. Juliette looked down at him, and nodded to herself as she walked into the kitchen. When she came back she was holding out a small envelope that had recently been ripped open.

'What is it?' I said.

'Came in the post this morning. Read it.'

I pulled out the tattered piece of paper, and as I unfolded it, Juliette's eyes watched me for a reaction.

On a small white postcard had been typed:

STOP DIGGING FOR TROUBLE. YOUR DIGGING IS ABOUT TO CAUSE YOUR FAMILY SUFFERING YOU CANNOT IMAGINE.

'Jesus,' I said. 'Who would have sent this?'

Juliette shook her head, disappointed by my response. '*So* many people Ben. The police, worried that their insufficient investigation could come back to haunt them? Someone at the school's board of governors? Paul Kraver?'

'It's Kraver.'

'Don't make this personal. You really think he'd risk it?'

'I don't think anyone else would risk getting caught. I'll get him for this.'

'Get who, Daddy?' Christian asked.

She shook her head, hard. 'Ben, is anger your only reaction? Why do you have to do the one thing we've been told not to do?'

'Well what would you have me do?'

As she kept shaking her head a kind of hysteria began to grip her. Her shoulders shook. I reached forward to hold her. Calm her.

'Juliette, stop it. Come on, it's okay.'

'No,' she said, pointing a shaking finger at me. 'I've already lost a daughter to these people and I'm not going to see them get my family again.' She fixed her eyes on me and began shaking her head. 'No. No,' she stammered.

'What do you mean? We have to fight this!'

'If you insist on fighting this, Ben, you won't be doing it under my roof. Not while filth like this is coming through my letter box!'

'What?'

'Ben, I've made a decision,' she said. 'This fight has become too vicious.'

'I agree,' I said, holding my hands out. 'This is probably the toughest time of our life, Juliette, right now. But, don't you see? This fight has to happen. We can't let another family go through what we've suffered out of fear of speaking out. We *have* to find out what happened.'

'I don't care about other families,' she said, firmly, closing her eyes. 'I care about what's left of mine. I am *not* letting you turn this home into a battle ground.' She firmly massaged a tuft of Christian's hair, which stood up defiantly after every stroke. With big eyes Christian looked between us. 'I couldn't control what happened to Marine, but I'm going to make damn sure Christian doesn't suffer as well,' she said.

'What are you saying?'

She kept her eyes shut.

'Ben, just for now, I think you should stay somewhere else.'

+ + + + +

That afternoon, the spell broke. I left the house, with just a few possessions in a holdall, sure that the world no longer possessed any magic.

I closed the door behind me, and waited for Juliette to rush outside and pull me back into the home we'd built. As I stepped down onto the street I gradually realized that she was not going to do that.

I was unable to think rationally, to consider what hotel I should stay in. I parked my car on the edge of the city, leaving my bag, and I walked, almost as if drugged, towards the lights of the town. I had hoped to spend the evening planning my strategy but I had more pressing problems now. I didn't know what to do, and some silent intuition had taken over.

It was that subdued part of the day – when the lights in cafes have been switched off, but before garish pubs illuminate the dark.

It was only during that walk that I started to see behind the scenes of real life. Walking on the bridge into the city I passed a man thumbing a battered acoustic guitar as he sang 'Waterloo

Sunset'. He was trying so hard to charm the blithe passersby with his tribute to another place, and to a forgotten time. Behind him, the water quietly shimmered. A harsh backdrop in which nothing was reflected.

As people passed him by, in a thick stream, I thought of the world as one huge tide. Each droplet within it another distinct person. It was a tide that heaved, building power and intent, before inexplicably falling apart, then starting to gather once again. Some waves congregated at the musician's feet, dropped money, and then were washed away. I saw then that people were just glad to be part of a wave, glad to be moving, glad to acknowledge that they were part of a sea. As the man turned into himself, blowing his hands against the cold, I wondered if people had to act in waves - to retain a sense of their own essence. At that moment the lone singer was divorced from the purpose of his sentiments. No one wanted to hear from them, and he knew it. His words rang out over an isolated river. He was a solitary drop, exposed enough to evaporate or be wiped away.

I stood over the river, at the place at which the bridge met the pavement and the city began. I peered over the edge into the darkness. Looking closely, I watched that silvery mass mix into itself. I moved closer to the edge.

The temptation to throw myself over, to have that swaying body anaesthetize me with the comfort of death, was so powerful.

I didn't want to fight any more. I didn't want to be separated from home. More than anything I had never wanted my family to be harmed. But it had been harmed, permanently. Now, by trying to fight for justice over that, I was causing them to be harmed even further. But what sort of a person would give in, and let them get away with it?

As I looked down at the river, I could see the wager. I could see the energy and fight and belief that I needed, to win. I knew, deep within my soul, that at that moment I didn't have what was required. I would lose the fight, but I would go down trying. The worst outcome possible was what would occur. Harder still, no one would lament my loss. They would say 'he was a fool for trying'. But I knew it would cause me such torment not to fight. Standing there I could see the whole torrid transaction still to come.

I stepped closer to the edge, the pain building up within me. Ready to break in a poisonous wave. Just jump, I thought. Jump, and soon it'll all be over. The uncertainty, the pleading, the planning, the pain.

My feet shuffled against the wall, as I worked out how to mount it. I momentarily thought of Christian. Of Marine, smiling. Her eyes laced with salt on that cool island beach. When pain was unimaginable. I pictured her expression. What would she say if she could see me now?

'Daddy, what are you doing?'

I stepped back, tears streaking my face. But the seductive power of the water seemed irresistible. I wanted it wrapped around me. I could jump, I thought, and it would at least buy me time. But Marine's smile flashed into my mind. 'No,' I said.

I rarely bothered to pray. I had only prayed once, when Marine was born. I had prayed for her to be protected by the universe. Even then it seemed a dumb request. Now the universe had rejected my plea I saw little point in praying now. But I did, standing there on the edge.

As I stood a step back I released a small prayer.

'I won't kill myself tonight,' I whispered. 'But if it gets any worse, then I will. I have lost it all. Give me something to stop me coming back to this bridge again.' I looked up at the sky, and saw that it was empty, and I pulled myself away from the edge.

My phone bleeped. Phillip.

I'm worried about you. And not just because you dress like a celebrity chef on a daytime chat show. Can you call me?

I laughed, gritted my teeth, and turned towards my car.

THIRTEEN

I COULD SEE, from his reaction, that I must have been hollow-eyed when I arrived at his flat.

'What Hammer Horror flick were they filming today then?' he asked.

'I can't look that bad,' I said, trying to swing my bag over his threshold.

'It's not you that's bad,' he said, with a soft smile.

I wasn't used to him being this accommodating, and I suspected it would be a fight for him to sustain it.

'What do you mean?'

He exhaled. 'I know Juliette is grieving, but I think throwing you out right now is pretty unforgivable. She should not be abandoning you. It's your family. Your house as well.'

'Only until we default on the mortgage in a month's time. She's ended it, Phil.'

'It will pass, you know that. Come on, get in here.'

'No, I don't know that. I don't know how to even begin to fix this situation.'

'You can begin by moving in here for a bit,' he said, frowning. He fished through his pockets, and handed me a set of keys. 'You always have a place, even if it is just a punctured futon. I bet you've come to the same conclusion as me about who sent that awful postcard?'

'I expect so,' I said.

He seemed to want to say something, but years of rivalry caused a blockage. A low buzz of anger emanated from his eyes. I had never seen it before. I saw then that there was an anger in Phillip regarding injustice in the world. But he seemed to struggle to find the words to express it. Except in his stand-up, perhaps.

'Thanks,' I said.

'Come on, Ben. Tonight, we're going to shake off your problems. I have just the ticket. We'll party like we're nineteen again.'

That evening Phillip was performing a one-off stand-up gig for charity in the City Hall. He'd put two tickets aside for Juliette and me and he insisted that I still use mine 'Can you meet Violet in town?' he asked. 'Give her Juliette's ticket? I want her to see my show. I think she'll like it.'

As I waited for Violet, by the statue of Neptune in the square, I wondered if Phillip had been right about Juliette. In a world of chaos, perhaps it is a bad gamble to commit to one person. One false turn and you can be left teetering on the gaping morass.

I took in the crowd. This shimmering shoal, winding their way past, sticking together. The windows of each shop appeared like glassy voids. Ready to suck the curious into their consumerist whirl.

This is life, I thought. Scattered with whirlpools.

FOURTEEN

'YOU LOOK FROZEN,' a voice said.

I looked up and recognized Violet, a stylish woollen hat pushing her fringe onto her eyelashes. As she leant in to hug me I took in her scent, and noticed the pastel blue nail varnish that clasped my shoulder. She was like a treasure-box of femininity, the lid askew enough to shed some of its gold light.

'We've got ages before the gig,' she said, taking in the swirling masses. 'What do you reckon, shall we get a drink?'

'We'll need it, if we're going to find Phillip funny for a whole hour,' I said.

She chuckled, and we moved into the throng.

The city now seemed submerged into its own essence, silver light reflecting off its windows and rivers. We trailed up a cobbled street and peered in at the slightly wonky bars, all full of the low murmur of intimacy and discretion.

'We could have a swift one in here,' Violet said, placing a clumsy mitten against a steamed window.

'Sure,' I said. 'Why this one?'

'Because I used to barmaid in here and the manager was dead sexist, talked down to me all the time.'

'But surely you want to avoid it then?'

She smiled, wanly. 'Nah. I fancy going in with a famous celebrity and seeing his reaction.'

'Glad to be of service,' I said.

She went inside, and I followed. Sure enough, the flinty exchange between Violet and the doughy man behind the bar suggested some smothered resentments.

'Let's get a couple of cocktails,' I said.

She nodded, and adjusted her hat. 'You sound like man trying to drown something?' she said as she peered, on tiptoes, at the contents of the optics.

'Or a man just trying to drink something,' I said.

'You sure about that?' she asked, tilting her head as she chose a drink. I wondered how much she knew, and how much she had intuited. There was something in her squirming, in the dogged determination to keep probing, that suggested sexual intensity.

We found a small booth at the back of the pub, where the slow advances of people in the lane outside were only just discernible. I had envisaged that evening that I wouldn't be able to socialize, but Violet's presence invigorated me. After our first meeting I had marked her down as vaguely pretentious. But what I had taken as pretension now seemed to be an admirable sense of aspiration.

'So, did you enjoy your *Almost Famous* moment?' I asked, as we set down the bright cocktails.

'You know, not as much as I thought I would. Perhaps because you're not famous enough. Maybe you need to go on Big Brother, or Celebrity Love Island. Raise your profile a bit.'

'One of those shows where they pair you up with some other D-lister in the hope of sparking a romance?'

'Nah, you're not D-List,' she said, mock-aghast.

'Just out of curiosity then Violet, where am I?'

'Well you're not A-list,' she said, taking a strong sip. 'Oh, that's pretty good. So A-list is like Tom Cruise. B list - I don't know, Ryan Giggs?'

'If you have to sleep with your wife's brother to reach the B list, I'm not interested.'

'Ha. C-list, Chris Evans? So, I'd say right now, you're stranded somewhere between B and C.'

'I had no idea I sat so high in the alphabet.'

She leant back, but her perfume closed around me. Its grip was strong. I suddenly had a very clear vision of Violet, focused as she worked behind the bar. Planning for something more, as she poured pints. Inspecting the world outside with narrowed eyes.

'You don't know how famous you are, do you?' she said.

'I can't be that famous. But what about you?' I asked. 'Was finding the lost pages of that diary all part of a grand plan to reach the A-list?'

She shook her head. 'I'm just trying to keep my chin above water,' she said. 'I was the first person in my family to even go to university. Doing this Masters is so far ahead of the plan that I'm just trying to keep going. You know, trying not be found out.'

'Wow. You must be smart. Or have worked incredibly hard.'

'Yeah. Both, you know,' she said, feigning nonchalance. 'But I'm sure you've worked hard to get to where you are too, Ben?'

'I suppose so.'

'And all you want is to know it's not in vain?'

'Yeah. Now more than ever,' I said.

'I sensed that,' she said, looking down at her drink.

'Why do you say that?'

She titled her head back. I noticed how her lips, falling into a natural pout, had a cherubic quality to them. Her eyes now seemed less curious, and more visionary. They betrayed within her something that I suspected had never been played out in the real world, and perhaps only fleetingly grasped in her own mind.

'The first time I met you, you looked pained,' she said.

'I'm still in the thick of something.'

Looking back, I can see how lacking in self-awareness I was at that moment. I should have realized that Violet was not only inquisitive, but resourceful too. At that point I didn't fill her in on Marine, and the trial, not because she was a stranger (as she felt simpatico) but because I didn't want to bore her. But I didn't realize what a powerful intrigue I had triggered in her by so blithely dismissing my own apparent problems and what she called my 'fame'. I should have known someone like Violet would become more determined to find out the true story. Sometimes, the universe hands you a lifeline and I got the sense just then, that Violet was it.

It felt good, in the low heat of that bar, to be able to ignore the dark clouds about Juliette, and the trial, as I bantered with this vibrant young woman. But the moment she got up to 'powder her nose' the miasma descended. This conversation is a little bubble, I thought, and it's about to break. She can't genuinely care about me, and I'd be a fool to hope for that.

The venue was packed. The city hall looked resplendent, with its pillars, wide staircases, and 1930s ushers. A mass of young people were inching themselves inside. Thick beards, lustrous hair, and whipped scarfs studded my eyeline. 'Phillip's show has sold out,' Violet said, looking at her ticket. We made our way to our seats, close to the front. 'It must be all those rumours about his set.'

With the chaos going on in my own life, I had barely paid attention to the news. I had caught, in passing, recent reports of extremist Islamic groups once more targeting newspapers that contained cartoons of the Prophet Mohammed. Some publications had drawn praise for their bravery, by responding to this extremist violence through printing the cartoons even more widely. Refusing to bow down to this extremist ideology.

I had an inkling that Violet was alluding to those rumours. The theatre was, indeed, full and the lights turned low as we waited for Phillip to appear. I thought how similar the stage seemed to a classroom. Onstage a mike stand and a table holding a bottle of water were bathed in gold light. Behind them a large white writing pad was propped up on an easel.

Phillip came onstage to Marilyn Monroe's 'I Wanna Be Loved by You'. He was wearing a creased blue dinner jacket that was far too large for him, and he flapped his hands in greeting as the audience applauded. A spotlight followed Phillip to the middle of the stage. As he adjusted the mike stand, and waved away the cheers, I noticed how he was now adopting a bumbling, staggering persona. It was fresh and yet, in flashes, pure Phillip.

'Thank you, thank you for having me,' he said, seizing the mike.

The audience quieted. His voice was much softer when he began to speak. 'When my agent asked me if I wanted to do a show in the North East, I said, "No, I don't want to do a show in the North East."

I noticed that he had adopted a lisp, to further exaggerate the sense of his incompetence. I found myself leaning forward, with the rest of the crowd.

'And my agent said to me, "Why don't you want to do a show in the North East?" and I said, "Listen to me, there's a very good reason why I don't want to do a show in the North East. Because I've heard it's horrible. And if it's anything like that Middle East..."' The audience started laughing. Smiling, Phillip said, 'I know, I know. So it seems to me like we are all on the same page, and you understand me, and I understand you.'

Violet leant against me. 'I feel nervous,' she said, her hand on my sleeve.

'Now I know what you're thinking,' Phillip said, closing his eyes, and patting an imaginary concern with his hands. 'You're thinking "this man clearly is a great intellectual, as well as a sexually powerful presence" - and you'd be right, you'd be right.'

More laughter.

'But I just want you to settle down and relax, because tonight I'm going to use my intellect to educate you about what is going on in the news. So.' He turned towards the white board. 'There's been a lot of issues in the news about people portraying the prophet Mohammed. And my job here tonight, ladies and gentleman, is to fix this mess once and for all. Using this pen.'

An icy gasp rose from the audience as he took a marker pen from his pocket and moved to the pad. He flicked the cover of it to reveal a clean white page.

'I know people have been getting very upset because they feel - and I quote -'

He took out a small crumpled piece of newspaper from his top jacket pocket and scrutinized it.

'I can't read exactly what it says because I left my contact lenses on the bus. But I'm pretty sure this article says that the Prophet Mohammed has been portrayed badly in cartoons.' He looked up, as people exchanged glances, chuckling. 'So tonight, ladies and gentlemen, I'm going to portray the Prophet Mohammed properly.'

As he pulled the lid off his pen there were a few nervous titters.

He turned to the audience, spreading his hands. 'Now there's no need to be nervous,' he said, with a tiny smile. 'What I'm saying is, let's look at organized religion in a responsible way. Let's admit we've got an issue in this country, with our attitudes towards other cultures. Let's admit that, please. Let's not argue. Let's have an adult debate about an adult topic, using a cartoon.'

'The thing the cartoons have often got wrong,' he said, drawing the face of a man, 'is they've not got Mohammed's features right. We're talking here about a great man, a wise man, a prophet. So he's going to have strong features.'

In hard, quick strokes Phillip drew bulging eyes, a large nose and a big mouth.

The audience gasped. 'I know, I know,' Phillip said. 'I'm sorting the situation out and don't worry, you can thank me later. By this time tomorrow Israel and Palestine should have sorted their differences out once and for all, and not before time. Anyway, I think another reason people think Mohammed is being portrayed badly ...'

'Oh God,' Violet said, laughing as she covered her mouth.

Phillip turned to the board and started to zigzag a large, zany beard onto his already inane caricature. The audience shuffled forward, hands clasped to mouths. A spike of laughter pierced the air.

We met Phillip at the after party, where he was being engulfed with well-wishers. They were a strange blend of angular young journalists, and mostly male comics. The comics all seemed to be exaggerating the nuances of normal personalities to try and make an impression. I was surprised by the pang of jealousy I felt as one cornered Violet, and asked her what she thought of the show. She said, 'It was nice to hear a comedian who doesn't just offer knob gags.'

'I know what you mean,' he said, looming over her. 'You don't want to pay money to have a man tell you all about his ablutions. If you wanted that you'd go into a gent's toilet and sit there with the toilet door open, wouldn't you?'

She winced. 'I'm not sure I'd handle any problem by hanging around a men's toilet,' she said. I sensed Violet's intellect was a trapeze on which this man was unknowingly being bounced. I found myself wondering what she was here for, why she had entered into Phillip's world, and mine by proxy.

'You alright?' I said, taking a can from a nearby table as Phillip moved over.

'Thank God you two are here,' he said. 'I feel like I'm playing the role of Simon Cowell in a shite comedy version of X Factor.'

'Interesting set,' Violet said. 'Half of it was funny and the other half just downright worrying.'

'Well, that's the reaction I hoped you'd have,' he said, cracking open a can.

'Glad to be of service,' she said, looking at him from the side of her eyes.

'Right,' Phillip said, looking between Violet and I. 'You two, meet me on the roof garden at Chaise Longue, in half an hour,' he said. 'I'll have to deal with the Greek chorus and then I can meet you up there.'

On the way to the bar Violet had clearly sensed a preoccupation in me. She took me wordlessly through the winding streets, to a black door, where a small sign signaled that we'd arrived. As I followed her inside I wondered how Phillip knew about this hidden place, a spacious bar decorated with retro plastic furniture, containing plenty of discreet corners. Synth music chattered quietly in the background as she led me through the sea of people, leather and jewellery shining on the cusp of each tide. We went up a narrow flight of stairs, opening out onto a roof garden. The high walls of the surrounding buildings framed the terrace, lined with rows of sofas. Glass tables housed teeming cocktails. Once we had our drinks, we weaved between fake palm trees to sit at one. On Violet's insistence I slowly unravelled the story of recent days. Once or twice I thought she might have blinked away a tear. As I described the hearing she seemed drawn into the story, and became part of its intense texture. I barely realized she had begun to press against me, her fingers subtly weaved into mine. When I finally said, 'And that's that,' she lapsed back into the chair, pulling our hands apart.

'What is it?' I said.

'You must fight this,' she said. 'Morally, you have no choice about the matter.'

'How so?'

'Because you have enough of a profile to get this scandal into the news. You know, get it dealt with. Have you ever heard that saying, 'All that is necessary for the triumph of evil is that good men do nothing'?'

I sipped. 'Yes. But have you ever heard the phrase "playing with fire"?' I asked.

I didn't know it then, but I was merely kicking the embers of her glowing curiosity. She nodded, her eyes fierce.

Phillip appeared in front of us at the bar, in an electric blue suit that fitted him snugly. He made a circling gesture and Violet raised a thumbs-up, agreeing to another round. When he sat down, Violet said, 'Ben's been telling me about his awful situation. If your show tonight was about anything—'

'Anything other than extremist terrorism?'

'Then it was about how entertainment can be used to make a serious point, to the masses.'

'The masses that fill comedy venues?' Phillip asked. 'Ben, have you ever thought about using your profile to speak out against what you're being put through right now?'

His anger is coming out again, I thought. He was able to express it onstage, through comedy, but finds it harder when talking about me.

'Exactly what I was saying,' Violet whispered, mixing her drink with a straw.

'How do you mean?' I answered.

'Art has been asking me again and again if you want to sign to him. In fact, he promised to call me in a few minutes to find out how the show went. He's yet to venture north of Watford Gap and actually see me perform. But why don't I pass him over to you when he calls?'

I looked over at Violet, who cocked her head at me encouragingly. 'Okay,' I said.

Over the course of the evening, Phillip was gradually surrounded by fans on the roof garden. My friend seemed to be a diffident Pied Piper amongst all the culture rats that scurried around him. He kept throwing looks at Violet, perhaps hoping for evidence that she was impressed. But Violet seemed oblivious to his glances. I had just become trapped in a conversation with a performance artist, who was elaborately telling me about her alter ego called Isobel, when I felt someone tug on my elbow. It was Phillip, holding out a mobile phone.

'Art,' he mouthed.

I nodded, and tried to find a quiet corner. There were none.

'How's it going?' I said, into the mobile.

'Ben! So you've finally come to your senses, I see. You know, there really is so much more you could be doing to capitalize on your profile.'

'I had no idea.'

'Such naivety! Beautiful. I am part of the second largest talent agency in the UK. So you couldn't be talking to anyone better. How about we get together to shoot the breeze this week?'

After the conversation, as I hung up the phone I turned to see Violet looking at me. Her expression suggested concealed amusement.

'You alright?' I asked.

'I'm going for a pint,' she said. 'Fancy it?'

'Sure. Just let me tell Phillip.'

'Phillip was last seen allowing a young female admirer to buy him a cocktail genuinely made from half a pineapple. We can catch up with him later,' she said.

'Okay,' I answered. 'You sure you don't mind him being left with someone like that?'

'I don't know what you're on about,' she said, standing still.

'It's just - I couldn't quite work out if there was something happening with you and him.'

She looked to one side. 'Nah, not at all.'

'I'm not sure that's how he sees it.'

'I just talk to people who seem interesting. That's all. Dead chatty, me.'

On the ground floor Violet blanched at the sudden influx of footballers, and the fur-lined coterie that breezed in with them. She texted Phillip to say we were going next door. I found myself wondering how honest she'd just been about her and my oldest friend.

We found a quiet corner in a mock-Tudor bar, next to a crackling fire. I bought our drinks and, having set them down, I pulled an armchair up next to hers. She smiled as she lolled her hands on top of my arm.

'You going to sign with this agent, then?' she asked.

I noticed that her long, sandy hair had stuck to the lapels of her coat. Its fragrance mingled with the heat of the fire, to create a seductive air.

'Looks like it,' I said, leaning into my drink.

Her eyes bobbed on my profile as I leant back. A delicate smile hovered on her lips.

'Don't you think that's dead exciting?' she asked, her fingers stepping over my arm. I looked sideways, the fire illuminating the strip of hair that had fallen from her left ear. It was a narrow white margin, laced with flames. 'Surely you see all the possibilities open to you right now, Ben? You could be a stand-up like Phillip. Use your media profile to pin those bastards down. Have a whole set about what they've done to you.'

'I don't think it would make for a very funny show.'

She lightly punched me, and then looped one arm through mine, and drew her lips close to my cheek. 'You know what I mean,' she teased. 'You could have a good crack at it.'

I glanced at her, flattered and confused by this sudden intimacy.

'Well, I think so, anyway,' she whispered. 'You could channel all this anger. You are in such a strong position.'

'You are the one in a strong position,' I said, reacting to the proximity. 'You're young, you're hungry to make something of yourself.' She smiled. 'You're beautiful too,' I said, 'which helps. Unfortunately, it's often only when people are older that they see all the potential they had. But you can achieve whatever you want.'

She looked past me. I wondered if her expression was guilty, somehow.

'Did I say something wrong?'

She frowned, her eyebrows drawing closer to one another.

'What is it?' I said. 'Did I say too much?'

A hand flashed up to her eyebrow. 'Nothing. It's just … I suppose you're saying some of the things that I say to myself, to keep myself going. But no one has ever said them to me before.'

'I'm surprised. You have to be careful though. People will try and butter up someone like you. To exploit them.'

'Yes,' she said. 'People do try and exploit one another. You need to watch out for that too, Ben.'

'It's happening to me already,' I said.

The remark made her sigh, as if she was surprised by the emotion of her reaction.

'I probably keep people at a distance, so they can't do that,' she said, quietly. 'But … something tells me I can let my guard down with you.'

'I don't know,' I said.

She flashed her eyes at me, mock-alarmed. 'No, what I mean is,' I said, sitting up, 'I have just the same frailties as any bloke. But, that aside, you probably have a greater capacity to achieve something than anyone else I know.'

'Coming from someone who's actually made an impact on the world, that actually means something,' she said. 'You know, when I watched those episodes of Educating Bristol I'd never seen someone talk so directly as you did to that girl. When you were coaching her to get through her GCSEs she had the same look on her face that I must have had when you complimented me just now. People generally just don't encourage and nurture each other. But for some reason you do.'

'Thanks.' I sipped.

'Which means you have the ability to fight this situation. And I think you can win. You've got the public on your side once already!'

I had a flash of realization, just then, that this was one of those fleeting moments in life. When all the formalities that have to be overcome, to allow someone to speak directly to you, have been traversed. One of those instants when someone, for once, was speaking so directly to my soul that I had no option but to absorb the nourishment of their observations. I could only see then how famished I was, how much I needed that sustenance.

'It's funny,' I said. 'But no one has said that to me before, either.'

'I feel sure that what I'm saying is true,' she said, with a sweet smile. 'I don't know how I feel so sure, but I do.'

It was such a relief to have someone identify these qualities in me that night that I almost broke down. I needed to hear that I had the strength to get through this. I understood then why people were so often defeated by this world. Perhaps the web of support that they required just did not come into alignment when it had to. Or perhaps our culture lacked the channels by which to offer this support. 'It means a lot to me to have you say that,' I said, looking up at her.

As I turned to her, the two of us were immersed in a cloud of intimacy that felt completely natural. Underneath that intimacy was a delicate throb of eroticism, a willingness on the part of this beautiful young woman to bear my burdens upon her own young shoulders. Somehow, Violet didn't see my burdens for what they were. She instead interpreted them as a somewhat thrilling challenge. I didn't know if that was because she had empathy, or because she lacked it. But she had already, in life, accrued the strength to take that weight onto herself.

As the emotions of the moment sank in I couldn't directly look at her. The effect of her proximity, femininity and kindness would, I knew, prove too potent for me to resist. To avoid looking at her, I leant in to her. She nuzzled her nose against the top of my head. The fire crackled, enhancing the sound of her sleeve moving, as she brushed a lock of hair from her ear. Violet sighed. Our faces began to turn to each other, I felt something in her yield.

'You look like you're going to kiss me, Ben,' she whispered.

I knew that in the shy smile of this young woman was the energy to defeat an army. 'You know I want to,' I said. 'But - I can't. It feels right, now. But in a day or so it would cause such pain to other -'

'I know. Then don't,' she said, her smile broadening.

Looking around she saw that we had the room to ourselves and she lay her long legs over mine. The flesh under her tights was softer, more fragile than I had somehow expected. Her fingers gripped mine, and the fresh buzz of her perfume made me feel weak. The fire, shining through her hair, seemed to illuminate a new future. It was an era that I knew we could usher in with a single kiss. Every time I looked at her she moved to kiss me. The fire raged, its tongues scorching the wood. Every time her face tilted to me, like a flower towards the sun, I thought of the pain I would cause to Juliette if I gave into temptation. Then there was a moment, when my mouth flashed over hers, and I resisted again. She smiled, bashful.

'Why do you think we are in each other's lives now?' she asked. 'Don't you find it a little sad that we can't do what we both want to do?'

'I agree.'

I looked down.

Violet's approach was slow, and even the sudden crack of the fire didn't dissuade her. She turned her face towards mine. As she did, I remembered that Juliette had pushed me away, and the memory stung. Violet kissed me tenderly, her hands resting on my lap. Both of us seemed to be restraining so much passion during that kiss, resisting the urge to push our bodies together. The urge to press myself against her was so pure and strong that I now felt cowardly resisting it.

'You don't need to feel guilty, Ben,' she said.

Violet's flat was on the first floor of a slightly dishevelled modern block. As she searched, at the front door, in her handbag for keys I was conscious of the illuminated apartments overhead, watching us. I had been surprised to hear myself accept her offer of a drink, but with there being so sign of Phillip I let myself go with the momentum of the evening.

Walking into her apartment was like stepping back in time, into a student era that I never got to fully imbibe the first time around. In her small, dimly lit hallway wooden racks were stuffed with paperbacks and laced with fairy lights. My eyes skittered over books about witchcraft, punk music, criminology. As I walked into the adjoining living room I saw the walls were decorated with posters of bands. Mick Jagger peacocked around on a stage, and Bowie stepped off a Berlin train, pensive and ambitious.

I sat on her sofa and watched her through the frosted glass boil a kettle in her kitchen. I shouldn't be here, I thought. I shouldn't be sat amongst the buttery scent of her living room, in the low light of this sanctum. I shouldn't be able to cast my eye over the black and white pictures of her, arranged carefully into diamonds on the wall. In which slender female friends wrapped their arms around each other in nightclubs. Why was she allowing me to feast on all this? For a moment I felt suspicious.

We drank tea, and as late night radio burbled from the kitchen, her legs began to enmesh with mine again. She rested her head on my shoulder. Even as I found myself pressed against the flesh of her thigh, this sequence of events felt natural. I felt as if for the first time in my life I had entered a landscape which I could identify as mine. One in which books and old records were the absorbent walls of an idiosyncratic life. I would gain sustenance from her intelligence, and indulgently help her whenever a kick of gratefulness happened to surge inside me.

'I should go,' I said, during a moment in which the candle of intimacy threatened to flicker out. I began to stand up, and she seized my wrists.

'Stay a little longer,' she said.

I nodded, and as if she was comforting someone, she pulled me into her. Our limbs found a way to receive each other and she kissed me. After the shock of the soft collision her mouth remained slightly open, as if she was stunned into submission. As I kissed her again, she began to rhythmically kiss me back, a sense of expression easing into our embrace. We pressed against one another, the proximity accelerated by lust. I suggested going into her bedroom. She nodded.

Entering Violet's room was like walking into a labyrinth of cultural references that had long glowed in my heart. There was a large Bob Dylan poster over her bed, in which a dark-haired woman grasped the troubadour's arm. A nest of flowers – pink and purple – filled the fireplace. As she busied herself in the bathroom, I took in the arrangement of concert ticket stubs and polaroids on the wall. I pushed a button on the bedside stereo, and soon Mazzy Star oozed from the speakers. The sound of thumbed acoustic guitars and low, sensual vocals absorbed the space. I could detect the scent of vanilla lip balm in the air of this elegant, feminine, netherworld. I moved to look at another array. It was a collage of pictures in which a caramel-skinned Violet was frolicking in a bikini.

'Checking out the pictures of me almost naked?' she asked, stepping lightly into the room in a white silk nightdress. She was barefoot, and the lightness of her steps made my heart quicken.

She poured us both a glass of wine, from the drinks tray by her bed. She handed me the vintage goblet and we took a gulp. Her eyes levelled with mine as we drank. She placed the glass on the floor as I set mine down, and she pushed me onto the bed.

'You should have just asked,' she said, straddling my waist. Violet pulled the thin white strap of her nightdress over her shoulders, to reveal the taut, blushing skin above her breasts. She lay against me and I felt a knife of pleasure surge through me. I caught a scent of roses as Violet looked down on me with her impatient hand unbuttoning my trousers. I noticed that her eyelashes were almost too long for her face.

With our clothes loosened, and her eyes blazing, she rolled onto the part of the bed exposed by the gathered duvet. She pulled me under the bed sheets. As I gathered the long flow of her hair, she took a deep sip of wine from the goblet on the floor. I admired the fine cut of her back, this sensual, subtle question mark, before she turned. Laying back down she unbuttoned her nightdress and without raising a hand I felt my heart thunder. With her swooping contours revealed, her warm body rested against mine, fingers stepping over my midriff. When she kissed me again a hunger rose in my mouth and she seemed familiar with the feminine need to yield to it. I pinned her to the bed, kissing her neck as she murmured in almost imperceptible agreement.

I eased my way down her body. 'Keep going,' she urged, her hips creasing the sheets as they bucked upwards.

The muscles of her stomach rippled with pleasure, the fine brown skin shimmering under the low light. Given her entreaty I was surprised at how slowly her thighs parted. My lips found the source of her pleasure, and Violet let out a low moan as I embraced her. I wondered how deeply she had been lost in books, as her moan was the sound of a distant tide crashing on an inevitable shore. Her fingers scrabbled through my hair, urging me to explore her more ravenously. My body responded, as I twisted in the sheets. At her insistence, I eased my body against hers. Her expression was one of beautiful compliance, a misty-eyed admission. Her fingers rested against my hips and her eyes met mine as I eased myself into her. I was surprised by her delicacy, and heat. She responding sensuously to my movement as she let out a low moan, widening her eyes as she draped a slim arm over my shoulder. Her eyes became transfixed on an interior landscape, and her sudden absence was sharply arousing. As she guided me, with one hand on my hip, I found the rhythm I wanted, savouring the sensations of her opening flesh. I willed myself to respond to her pleasures, and in the instant that I did she clenched her arms around me. She kissed me, the tingling shock still present in our mouths. She seemed desperate to keep up the contact between our lips. She drove me on, her fingers clamouring at my back. The sudden contraction of her belly made her cry out as she was rocked by an orgasm that seemed at once knife-like and satisfying. Looking up at me, her eyes glowing decadently, I urged myself into the exquisite geometry of her neck and thighs, encouraged by the gentle entreaties of her hands on my back. It was the wildest, most outrageous indulgence, to find the nuances of my own pleasure inside her body. As I did I had the sudden sense that I was drinking greedily from a fountain. The sheer gratefulness that bubbled through me was hard to contain. The sudden, hot-mouthed embrace, combined with a sudden bucking of her hips made my body shatter.

I awoke at three in the morning. A thin wave of cold air was shimmering through a gap at the window. Violet was a voluptuous crescent in the sheets next to me, breathing softly. I rolled onto my back, and exhaled as quietly as I could. A powerful sense of self-loathing bloomed inside. I felt as if I had torn something that I would never be able to perfectly stitch up. It would always sit there, a high scar on my flesh. I quietly wondered if I had lost my family forever.

'You alright?' Violet whispered, turning over.

The morning light revealed a light spattering of freckles on her nose. 'I hope so,' I said, 'after what I've just done.'

She caught her breath. 'Don't talk about me like I'm an accident, Ben,' she said.

FIFTEEN

MY FIRST MEETING with Art took place two days later.

Juliette and I had exchanged brief, terse texts in the interim. They related purely to the enquiry and suggested that she clearly wasn't about to invite me home. In a strange way I was glad, because I hadn't yet been able to process what had happened with Violet. To try and make sense of it all, I continued to walk numbly around the city during the intervening days. I was sure that with enough concentration I could formulate a plan to figure it all out. But the city seemed like a set of narratives that didn't form a story; a set of cultures placed uncomfortably close to one another. Its muggy streets and urban wastelands offered me no solace. No matter how many times I tried to solve the complex equation of my life there was always some parts of the formula left unblended.

I'd return back to Phillip's flat hot and flustered. He'd usually be watching a comedy DVD, a tumbler of whisky in one hand. He didn't enquire about what happened with Violet on the night of his show. I suspected he thought I had made my way back to his place without her. But his assumption that Violet wouldn't be interested in me, and that I was too blindly loyal to Juliette to be interested in her, still smarted.

On my third night there we were watching a Clint Eastwood Western when he looked up from his phone and told me Violet would be joining us. As the TV screen flickered I silently wondered if he had asked her over, or if she had invited herself. I hoped that I wouldn't give myself away when she arrived.

Violet didn't seem to have any such qualms. The subdued, dimly lit room became less sombre the moment she entered. She keenly accepted Phillip's offer of whisky. Phillip's eyes played on the back of her head as she kissed my cheek in greeting and sat down on the sofa next to me. Philip threw himself into the armchair in front of the television. The three of us sat watching the screen, as the bottle of whisky on the table was slowly drained.

'When did you two meet?' she asked, looking between us.

'We were roommates at university. Though Ben spent more time in the library than in our room.'

Violet smiled kindly at me.

'And Phillip spent more time in bed than in the library,' I said.

'You were a lazy student?' she asked him.

'He's referring to the amount of time I spent chasing women,' Phillip said.

'You fancied yourself as a lothario?' she asked. 'I can't imagine you being one, somehow.'

'Oh yes,' I heard myself say. 'Phillip had a different woman every week.'

Phillip shot me a look. 'That's a bit of an exaggeration. There weren't that many women. It's just Ben wasn't very good at telling them apart.'

'You two obviously go back a long way,' she said. 'Moving back here must be like being at university again!' she said.

'In so many ways,' I answered, glowering.

'Except now,' Violet said, dangling her glass, 'Ben has every right to feel a little more confident of himself.'

I shot her a glance, but she seemed to enjoy the look of panic on my face.

As Violet nursed the remains of her tumbler, Phillip and I scoured the drinks cabinet in the kitchen for any booze we'd overlooked.

'Feel free to get an early night, if you want,' he said. 'I know you'll want to be fresh as a daisy for our trip to London tomorrow.'

'You're coming with me to meet Art?' I asked.

'Of course,' he said. 'Didn't your parents ever tell you to always introduce strangers to one another?'

'That's good of you,' I said. 'But I can't go to sleep just yet. I need to let the alcohol do its work first.'

'No problem,' he said. 'It's just - I wouldn't mind having a few minutes alone with Violet.'

He peered through the crack in the door, where Violet's heels were just visible on the table. 'I think tonight might be the night,' he said. 'I sometimes really think I can imagine her taking Christine's place.'

'You don't think that's asking too much of her?'

'Why do you say that?' he asked.

'No reason,' I said.

+ + + + +

As the lush, wet countryside streaked past the train window I closed my eyes and sat back in the seat. The heave of forward motion had shaken up a sense of nauseating hollowness. What was I doing? Taking career advice from an intense university student, and a provocative comedian? Was I really now expecting a celebrity agent to offer the solution to my situation?

I had a strong desire to get off at the next stop. To go home and to try and beg the school, and Juliette, to take me back. I missed Christian and Juliette ravenously. Missed having her body curled up against mine, and his dismissive chuckle. It seemed to make much more sense to let the enquiries run their course, and in the meantime to focus simply on staying away from the bridge. But it was a couple of emails, which until then I had not yet read on my phone, which changed my mind.

Over the last few days I had realized that I needed to message some former colleagues about retrieving my possessions from work. Their responses, which came belatedly, surprised me. The first email that I opened, from Colin, mentioned matter-of-factly that my desk had been cleared, and that an agency-appointed member of staff was now taking my class.

I felt unable to type a response. I could not believe how ruthlessly Kraver had prised me from my job. Even at my most cynical I hadn't expected the final line of the next email I got:

Kraver told us to not expect you back.

I hadn't expected an outpouring of loyalty from the other teachers. But I was not prepared for the blitheness of their responses either:

'Sorry to hear it hasn't worked out. All the best.'
'You'll bounce back mate. These things happen.'

These were people who I had rushed to help when they had found a class too difficult to manage. People who'd later hugged me and thanked me for supporting them, who'd told me they'd 'always be there for me' if I needed them. Who had praised me, privately and publicly, for my teaching methods.

Given the sense of comradeship I had felt during the most challenging days of teaching, this galled me. I knew, deep down, that I would never have allowed Kraver to trample over any one of them like this. I started to suspect that Kraver had sent a missive out to all of them, frightening them into not contacting me. Kraver would have known that if the teachers joined together his accusations would soon buckle under serious scrutiny. His plan had worked. I was now not only isolated from my job, and my family, but from my colleagues too. All I had was Phillip and Violet – and even that dynamic was fragile enough to break following a single indiscretion.

'You having doubts?' Phillip asked, from the seat opposite. He'd worn a suit for the occasion, and it looked like he hadn't slept.

I shook my head. 'No. Not at all,' I said.

$$+ + + + +$$

'Phillip has described you as "a good man in free fall",' Art said, leaning over a clear glass desk opposite us.

His face evoked a cartoon goblin. This impression was enhanced by the half-moon spectacles perched on his nose. Art's appearance, ironically, created the sense that he must be honest to have succeeded in spite of such a comically mischievous image.

'Is this a good description of you?' he asked. His voice, with its Hollywood pretensions, seemed to pinch, raising an octave as it sharpened towards a question.

Art's office was a world away from the cramped classrooms that I was used to. The clean glass and smooth chrome suggested any purpose could be directly achieved, if he was inspired to try.

I looked sideways at Phillip, who carefully placed his fingertips together. We were five floors up, and through the clear glass behind Art, I could see London. Spinning, bickering, manoeuvring.

'I think I am honest. But it can take only one transgression for you to start to wonder,' I said.

'Transgression?' Art was savvy enough to know that such a comment revealed hidden secrets. 'So, if you have transgressed at all I need to know now,' he continued, 'so we are prepared if it gets used against you. Believe me, Ben, they'll be rooting around in the dirt as we speak.'

Phillip shot me a look. 'Take it from me,' he said, 'Ben has not transgressed. If he's told to not walk on the grass, he forgets grass exists. There's nothing they can get him on. Right, Ben?'

I looked at my hands.

Art looked between the two of us. 'Really, Ben? So I'm assuming here you have no gambling habits, drug addictions, or exotic mistresses that we need to know about? Am I right?'

I looked at the floor. 'Yes,' I said. 'As a teacher I always gave it all I had. My own reputation, my own 'Fitness to Practice,' was only ever questioned after I had raised concerns about the schools enquiry.'

Art looked over at Phillip. The half-crescent glasses jumped as he crinkled his nose. 'Okay,' he said. 'Because these are the only snags that could, you know, hold us back here.' He shuffled the papers in front of him, and I guessed at a furtive mental calculation going on in his brain. 'So I think we've covered the major considerations,' he said. 'And I am grateful to you, Simon, for your counsel.'

Phillip had proposed I use his lawyer. I had almost forgotten he was sitting in a corner behind me. Our debate about whether to employ him had been a short one - I had argued that his costs would cripple us and Phillip had firmly said I had no choice. Simon Bracewell had joined the meeting late, but with enough confidence to suggest he was well-prepared. The learned air offered by his grey curls was offset by a slim, almost muscular physique. As I looked at him I was reminded of that John Major quote, when he spoke of an England composed of 'long shadows on cricket grounds, warm beer, invincible green suburbs'. Bracewell seemed to be a product of that retreating world.

'My pleasure,' Simon said, nodding. 'It looks as though you have a very strong case, Ben. You can, by all means, now make your predicament public. If you talk to the media using the language we agreed, the school can't *successfully* sue you. But there is one condition. We have to be able to argue–'

'Not argue - prove,' Art said.

'My apologies. *Prove* that you have exhausted all available complaint procedures before you make the matter public.'

I shuffled in my seat. 'Juliette spoke to the school's statutory body yesterday,' I said. 'She told them that we're planning to submit a formal complaint about Kraver's bullying. But they told her that they could not consider such a matter while I am answering questions about my Fitness to Practice.'

'Excellent,' Art said. 'So, can you see what my face is doing right now?' He smiled, an act which comically lowered his nose. I laughed. 'That's right,' he said. 'Now, why might I be smiling, Ben?'

'Stop showing off,' Phillip said.

I turned to Phillip. 'You're the biggest show-off in the world,' I said.

'Art has a right to feel confident about this,' Bracewell said, moving his chair in line with Phillips. 'Because Kraver has now done everything possible to prove that this is a classic case of an employer targeting a whistleblower.'

'A whistleblower?' I asked.

Bracewell nodded. 'That is what you are now, Ben,' he said. 'You have blown the whistle on the cover-up around Marine's death and as a result you are now in the latter stages in 'The Life Cycle of a Whistleblower'.'

'You'll have to explain what you mean,' I said.

'Ever heard of Patients First?' Bracewell asked.

I shook my head.

'It's an organization set up to defend people who've blown the whistle on dangerous practices in the workplace, and then seen themselves harassed as a result. Have a read of this on the way home,' he said, handing me a double-sided print-out. 'This article explains how right now you are experiencing a backlash for simply blowing the whistle against an employer with something to hide. I've become pretty familiar with this story in recent times, Ben. I'd say that you were at Stage 23 by now. Where employers "spread the word that the employee will not be coming back"?'

'They have,' I said.

'So what's our next step?' Phillip asked.

'The next step is for you to officially sign me as your agent,' Art said, walking round the desk. 'Done, and dusted. Then, over the next few weeks, we prepare to share your story, on national television.'

I sat up straight. Phillip, his fingers immovable, seemed unmoved.

'National television?' I said. 'I thought you were just going to try and raise my profile.'

'Ben,' Art said, standing over me. 'The one tiny little detail Kraver hasn't factored in, is your public profile. He has probably decided that if you do speak out in the news he can use that to strengthen his argument, and say you are unmanageable.'

'Either that, I thought, or he has decided Ben doesn't have the guts to make the matter public,' Phillip said. I winced. 'Sorry,' he added.

'Don't you want to finally start to get ahead of him?' Art asked.

'I do.'

'I am going to get on the phone to Craig Peterson, and see if I can get you a slot on his Saturday night show,' Art said.

'This Saturday?'

He laughed, dryly. 'Well, I'll see what I can do. Don't worry, we are going to prep you every step of the way.'

'And I'll be by your side too,' Phillip said. 'Wondering why my agent hasn't got me an interview on that show, yet.'

Art ignored the dig. 'He's a big fan of "Educating Bristol", this Peterson,' he said, folding his arms. 'He's got the biggest viewing figures of any talk show right now, and he'll be over the moon to bag the first interview with you since 'Bristol' went stellar.'

'You really think he'd be interested?' I asked.

Art nodded. 'He'll ask about "Educating Bristol", some of its funny moments,' he said. 'But I will make sure he has a good enough stretch to question you about Marine.' He removed his glasses, squinting at the thought of something. 'At that point in the interview you do have to grab the reins, Ben. Tell him the rumours about this David Walker, about you pushing Katy Fergus to testify to the school's enquiry. About how they whitewashed what really happened on the day Marine fell. Your meeting with Kraver, and this whole Fitness to Practice debacle.'

'Yes,' Phillip said, gripping the arms of his chair and nodding.

'At that moment we turn the whole spotlight from you, onto Kraver. Bam.'

'Jesus,' I said, looking at the ceiling.

'Ben?' he said. 'Look at me.'

I focused warily on the quivering man before me. 'You do what I am telling you and you will dismantle Kraver's case in a matter of minutes.'

'I like the sound of that,' I said.

'Your suspension will be lifted and your money problems–'. He feigned an explosion with his hands. 'Boom. They'll be gone. *If* you do exactly as we say.'

'I will give it my very best shot.'

'You do understand that when you are on the show you need to be charismatic, angry, and articulate, all at once?' Art said.

'That could be a problem,' Phillip said.

'I take it you're joking,' Art said, a little testily.

'He's got a point, actually,' I said. 'When I get nervous, I clam up,' I said.

Art shook his head.

'You will speak,' he said. 'Or you will lose everything.'

SIXTEEN

JULIETTE TEXTED ME that evening, asking when I would be home. As I drove through the city, I felt as if I was approaching a graveyard, in which our joint ambitions had begun decaying.

The city was cool that evening, and along the coastal road children trailed on bikes, along the path overlooking the sea. The ocean was a calm, flat blue surface, and I felt unable to pull any emotion from my surroundings. I needed an injection of belief before I could return home and continue the fight. But guilt sagged in me. How could I argue for my right to return home, when I had betrayed Juliette's trust? As I drove, following the smooth horizon of the sea with my eyes, I realized that any comfort I had derived from Violet, any anger I had felt against Juliette, was nothing in comparison to the permanent guilt I would now be living with. If I was to admit what I'd done I to Juliette I would be inflicting her with more pain, just to assuage my own guilt. But if I was to keep it secret I would be allowing a wound to fester, that would destroy any joy of living. I had made a mistake, but I couldn't confess it. But even more worrying, Violet seemed to have started to play an important role in my life. But there was no way I could say that, and admit to have felt something for her.

I watched gulls, circle overhead, ready to pick at any abandoned remnants they could find. I knew that soon karma would catch up with me, and then I'd be rightly left out in the cold. Picked at by anyone who bothered to address me. I needed, on that drive home, to find the courage to allow me to face up to the days ahead. But guilt flattened me, and indecision almost made me ease my foot from the accelerator and turn towards the sea.

I drove the car to the end of our street, sun flashing in the windows of each of the houses before ours. In them I saw a glancing image of Marine, dancing. I parked, tried to shake the image from my head.

I let myself in through the front door, moving lightly upstairs. As I eased inside Christian rushed up to me, silently. I picked him up, and inhaled his scent. I felt so consumed with love for this fragile mix of bones and flesh – the only remaining mixture of Juliette and me. I promised myself that I would never leave him again. I looked up and saw Juliette, standing a few feet back. She noted the ferocity in my embrace of our son, and I felt ashamed.

As Christian played with a toy crane at our feet, I told Juliette about the meeting in London and the plan that had been developed. Our bodies mirrored one another as we sat on opposite seats, hunched. As I spoke, I looked carefully for her reaction. To my relief, I saw that she was starting to nod. When I stopped talking the silence in the room came as an undeserved balm.

'I have been thinking about what we can do as well,' she said, her voice almost a whisper. 'I have been talking to your colleagues. They are more supportive than you realize.'

I looked up. She kept nodding, her thoughts gaining momentum.

'Kraver called them all into the staff room the day after he threw you out, you know. He told them that they would be "undermining the cohesion of the school" if they got in touch with you. *That* is why you've heard so little from them. Everyone's scared.'

'I see,' I said.

'All except one,' Juliette said. She stood up, and sat on the sofa next to me. She placed her hand on top of mine, and the energy of this gesture sparked my body back to life.

'You, you mean?' I said.

She smiled. A couple of new lines had appeared at her eyes. 'Well, yes,' she said. 'But also Lorraine Hannerty. She thinks Kraver is hiding something big. I convinced her to collect some information about him. Some testimonies from the other staff, about their view of the situation. I had no idea you were planning to go on national TV, but I – I was trying to be useful.'

'Juliette,' I said. 'You are much more than just useful. It is going to be one hell of a fight. But if we're going to win, I really think we need to be a team from now on,' I said.

'I know,' she said, a small fire burning in her eyes. 'I am sorry I reacted the way I did.' She looked directly at me. 'I really admire how you have never stopped fighting for Marine.'

'I've made some mistakes too,' I said.

'I know,' she whispered, standing up.

She stood there for a second, and I wondered what else she was going to say. But then she moved to the kitchen, and switched on the taps. I listened to her fill a glass, and I exhaled.

+ + + + +

I was torn between wanting Art to call, and hoping that he never would. The next day he rang just as I was about to shower. In a yelping voice he told me that in two and a half weeks I would indeed be interviewed on the nation's favorite talk show. Just as I was digesting this news he also told me that in a few hours I would have 'the honour' of being paid a visit by a 'thrusting young publicist called Emilia, who will give you a crash course in being on TV'.

'Some teenager is going to be telling me how to sit up straight in my own home?' I asked.

'She's just brilliant,' he said. 'They say you can't polish a turd, but this girl could wrap it in enough glitter that it sparkles under the spotlight.'

'I see,' I said.

'I'm not saying that, publicity wise, you're a turd. Of course not, Ben. But she'll polish you 'till you sparkle like the Fourth of July.'

I responded to the news of this impending visit by rushing into the bathroom, as a hot surge of poison rose in my throat. I hacked it into the bowl. The act of ejecting it made me so dizzy that I stayed in there, clutching the towel rail.

Juliette rushed in, her arm snaking around my shoulder. 'What is it?' she whispered.

'There's no way I can do it,' I said. 'I'll end up vomiting in front of millions of people.'

'Don't worry,' she said. 'It will all happen one step at a time.'

Emilia's arrival was preceded by a flurry of unpunctuated texts through to my phone. She asked about parking, told me her driver was lost, and then told me the matter was solved all before I'd had the chance to reply. Moments later, I answered the rap at the door to be greeted by the sight of a Tasmanian devil wrapped in a pashmina.

Emilia spoke in the excessively sensual tones of a public school girl raised to overpower people. She placed me in a wicker chair by the window, and barked questions about my early life.

Her first interjection came only a few questions in. 'This,' she said, mocking my crossed legs and hunched shoulders, 'makes you look like you've just backed your car onto your neighbour's poodle.' She pumped her fist. 'Make it look like you have a spine in your back. Nice clear breaths, and project. Your mumbling would be fine if you were a cokehead in a shambling indie band. But if you're going to convince the nation you've been wronged, we need some vim.'

'I don't want to end up doing all those cheap politicians' tricks. Staring straight at the cameras, gesturing with a thumb.'

'I'm not trying to turn you into JFK,' she said. 'I don't think even I could do that in an hour.'

'Why don't I try and cook an omelette at the same time, as well?'

'Don't take the piss, sweetheart,' she said. 'You're a long way off getting on a primetime cookery show. Right, let's go again.'

I wanted to just focus on preparing myself for the interview, but my thoughts kept straying to the upcoming hearing. Letters would come through about it on a regular basis, but all of them were frustratingly light on any content. Each letter hid its meaning behind a web of bureaucratic language. Having read the first five I realized that Kraver wasn't actually trying to offer me any information about the hearing through them. He was leaving a paper trail. I couldn't work out why he wanted to leave a paper trail, and I didn't raise it with anyone because I feared what the answer would be. He still felt a few steps ahead, while I was just lacing up my boots.

From then on, the interview with Craig Peterson was no longer my main concern. I had a hearing to prepare for, which would happen three days before I went on TV. I told myself that it was the hearing that would *definitely* shape the course of my life.

SEVENTEEN

WHEN I CAME HOME that night, after another evening of preparation, the house was dimly lit.

On my way home I'd had a text from Violet, asking when we could meet. Her direct choice of words played on my mind. It felt risky to tell her that I couldn't see her. What if she turned angry? What if she then told someone about our night together, who used it against me? I needed her support, but I couldn't keep her too close either. But what would she do if she felt at arm's length?

I dropped my bag on the floor, and called out for Juliette. My voice echoed around with an almost garish resonance. I felt as if I was screaming in a graveyard.

I could hear a peculiar scratching sound in the living room. Like someone was trying to get in.

I followed it, hearing it grow as I moved. The room was dark, and the window to the city was open. The thin white curtains around the frame appeared to billow in and out of the illuminated skyscrapers on the horizon. The scratching was coming from the side of the window, where Juliette appeared pressed against the wall.

When Juliette didn't answer, I wondered if Violet had rung the house. If Juliette already knew. But as my feet stepped closer to her, I saw that she wasn't ignoring me but that her attention was occupied. She was drawing on the wall, a large red crayon etching onto the brittle white surface the outline of a woman crouching. Hunched. As if shielding herself from invisible blows.

When she heard my footsteps she dropped the crayon with a clatter and rose to embrace me. When I took her in my arms her body felt ready to disintegrate. I made her see my eyes. She twice moved to hug me and I gently eased her gaze back to my face until she softly nodded. Then she grasped me, and her desperation was so great that I did not know what to do with it. I realized that I was not simply a person on a mission to get justice, but that I also needed to bring my Juliette back to life too. I had to do something, to make some change in her world, to allow it to all make sense for her once again. Otherwise, I knew that soon her flesh would crumble before me. I thought of Marine, cold in the ground, and the thought of her mother lying down beside her. The threat seemed very real, and the fight ahead very clear.

As she wrapped her body around me, I tried everything I could to let my soul fill my arms and torso and limbs, to rejuvenate her, but her soul was too crushed, and her darkness beat me. Some bleak spirit had taken hold of her, and somewhere within her frail flesh I could feel it whipping around, with a confidence that I could not combat. As I held her in my arms I felt the void inside her, and my tears began to fall. Her thighs closed around my back as I stood firm on the floor. The soft lilt of her sobbing mingled with the stirring of the lunar curtains. Through them a vast beam of moonlight projected into the house. I felt as though Juliette was trying to drink something from me. She held me in the way that an animal holds onto its parent in the wild. My tears began to gather on her shoulder but she did not move.

'I haven't been able to sleep this week,' she said.

I moved her onto her the couch, where she lay on her back. 'It's my fault,' she said. 'Listen to me. I pushed you away. It's my fault.'

Her body fit into the groove in the couch, and as she drew the lounge blanket around her I closed the window to prevent the chill getting to her. By the time I had returned to the couch, Juliette had closed her eyes.

'I keep having the same dream,' she whispered.

'Go on,' I answered.

She paused. 'You remember that nursery rhyme I used to play her on the piano?'

'Yes.'

'That's how the dream begins. I'm too tired to even cry and then I hear those chords in my mind.'

I closed my eyes.

'I played that song to Marine, because it was a happy sound,' she murmured. Her lips, pale and dry, kept moving. 'The melody reminded me of my grandma, singing it to me when I was a girl. As soon as I hear it I picture Marine. The two of us sat at the stool at the front of the piano. She's on my lap, and her fingers are mimicking mine as they move over the keys in time to the song. Her voice is one step behind the notes. And I slow down so that she can keep up but Marine slows down even further so that she is always behind the melody. And every time, I start to think that it is me that must be wrong, and so I concentrate on my hands even harder. And as I get more and more confused the keys start rising out of the piano. I can see the sides of them, and as they shift round they become steps. The steps to a giant slide. In the fairground.'

Juliette opened her eyes. But she was not looking for my reaction, instead moving through her own internal ritual. I am part of an inner audience, I thought.

'The fairground? Where I used to take her?'

'Yes.'

'But you never came with us,' I said.

She closes her eyes and I see them flicker under the lids. The side of my hand grazes her face and her fluttering eyelashes settle. 'I know,' she says, her speech again taking on that slow, dreamlike cadence. 'I couldn't come. I was always busy in the house. And also … I was scared. I was scared of taking Marine onto one of those rides, and of something happening to her. But in my dream you're always somewhere in the background. This time I've taken her onto the rides. I've taken her on the carousel, and I'm sure we've even gone on the dodgems. But that isn't enough for Marine. She wants to go on this towering giant slide. Where children disappear into the top and only come down a long minute later. And it's decorated so beautifully, this slide, that I think "what could go wrong?" It even looks like a delicious stick of candy. And at the foot of it Marine is clutching the mat, and tugging at my hand. "Mum, I'm going on this one," she says. Deep down I know I can't stop her. I curl some of her hair over her ear, but really I am touching her just in case it is the last time. Cherishing the feeling. "Don't go," I whisper and I hold her in my arms. I gather her up with all my strength and I hold her. Wanting to absorb her. "But I want to go on the slide," she says. I beg her, and hold her as firmly as I can. I try to take in enough of her scent that I can remember it. And I say, "Please, Marine, not today." And she says, "Please Mummy, I want to go." The next thing I know I can feel her breaking out of my arms.

I see her small head go up the steps of the slide. Then she turns, and waves. Her head is just visible through the slats but as she gets higher I can barely see her. She is so far up that she is almost in the clouds. I try to spot her, to note the moment that she has disappeared into the slide so I can follow her invisible journey down. I wait at the opening, but she doesn't come out. It is empty. I panic. I shake. I start to shout up at the slide. I wonder if she is waiting just inside for a joke. I hold onto this belief and I shout for her to get out.

Then, I start to crawl inside the tunnel. As I shout her name it goes black. So dark that I can't see a thing. The air tightens. I crawl and crawl and crawl. Until her name fills my ears, and it deafens me and then ...'

'Then what?'

'Then I wake up.'

She opens her eyes. Her gaze is completely impassive. I wrap my arms around her. Suddenly her body springs to life, the sickness leaves her, and a clean force surges through her, that I have not felt for a long time.

She holds me so tight that I think I wonder if I will permanently carry the imprint of her grief.

Somehow, I also begin to feel recharged. Juliette and I have connected again.

I tuck her into bed. Making sure that the duvet ends at her chin, so no cold waves chill her in the night. As I leave the bedroom my foot knocks against a cardboard roll, leaning against the doorway. I bend down to pick it up. See that it is full of large thick sheets of white paper. Careful not to make a sound I move into the kitchen, pull out the rolls and lay them out on the work surface. They are pictures of Marine. But this time they are not pictures of her bright outline, blazing around the page. This time the reds that shape her have cooled to oranges, mixed in with heavy blues - and this time Marine is lying down. Asleep. Around her, black circles press her into her resting place. Something inside me splits wide open.

Afterwards, I go into the bathroom and close the door carefully behind me. I think of the promise I made to Marine at the fair, and the one she made to me. How I knew, even at that age, that she would have grown into a woman who would have thought for her family as I would for her. The thought makes me start to shake, before my body collapses beneath me. My knees smash against the tiles and my head strikes the side of the sink. I fall into a clumsy, desperate prayer. I want to bury myself into the tiles of the bathroom floor and never feel this pain again. I realize how delusional I was to have any hope of building our family up again. With Marine gone, with Juliette lost and with my resolve weaker than ever I am sure there can be no way out of this.

I try and follow the wild shapes of my limbs as they struggle on the floor. I fear that I have lost my mind. Questions stab my brain, each gouging at me before they draw out of the tissue. What is a family made of? What does a father even do? He works, he brings home money, he is the final sea wall. But what the hell does any of that mean?

I look at myself in the mirror. My eyes are red, my skin is blotchy, and my belly is creeping over my belt. I am a joke. But as I pitifully study the reflection in the mirror an answer comes to me. I don't know where it comes from, but all I know is that at that moment I need an answer more than ever. The realization is that everyone needs to believe one person in their life is insurmountable. Right now, I have to be that person for Juliette. More importantly, I see that I can be that person. I will struggle, I will lie, I will beg and I will scrape. But I will play that role as fully as I can.

I understand then that a family is made up of small blocks – routine, intimacy, fun, and many other units. I now have to build up our idea of a home using those units. The mortar between the bricks is love, however difficult it might sometimes be to understand that. The blocks are stuck together by a heartfelt desire to make everyone happy and safe. I promise myself that tomorrow, I am going to start building our family up again. Brick by brick, unit by unit. Applying colour where I can. Perhaps one day, Juliette will join me in doing this. But I know that the first step is to get justice for Marine.

I look in the mirror and force a smile onto my face. I shake myself down and tread my way back to the bedroom. To the sleeping body of my partner.

EIGHTEEN

AT THE HEARING even the panel seemed to lack belief in my guilt. In a prefabricated first-floor room I sat in a chair, Bracewell on one side of me, nursing a surprisingly thin folder. I realized that I had no idea what we would have to pay him.

Before being called in I had waited outside with Phillip, who smelt a little of booze. Even Juliette, usually immaculate, had thrown on too much makeup. She seemed overwhelmed; her voice was hoarse and dry. The whole set up had the feel of a poorly arranged role-play. The frantic movement of staff members in the corridor, as we waited, revealed that they too were off-script. This in turn undermined their sense of authority. At the allotted time a wan receptionist ushered us into the room and I entered carefully.

Kraver sat with two other staff members that I vaguely recognized on either side of him. They were awkwardly seated on one side of a table placed in the centre of the room. A portly man at Kraver's left exchanged a glance with the drawn, dark-haired woman at his right. I sat opposite them, Bracewell lowering himself down carefully next to me. I decided that Kraver represented the only ballast of intent between the three of the panel members. His features seemed hardened, as if he'd been carefully rehearsing every aspect of this in his mind. Even his silence seemed prepared. His waistcoat - a bright shade of plum - was half-unbuttoned.

'My n-name's Alistair Robertson,' stuttered the larger man. He waved at the woman, 'and this is Valerie O'Donnell,' he said. He mopped his brow. 'As you k-know, Ben,' he began, his voice strangely sotto voce, 'we are here th-this morning to discuss some c-concerns that have come up about your conduct at the school.'

Anticipating my reaction, he raised a finger. 'N-now you know about these concerns from the advance letter you were sent.'

'No, I'm afraid I don't,' I answered. 'The letter just mentions "my behaviour on site", but doesn't specify exactly which behaviour was a problem.'

Robertson flashed a glance at Kraver, who appeared unmoved. Kraver passed a letter to Robertson, who briefly studied it. He flashed it at Bracewell and me. 'Here we have the letter as evidence that we have given you fair warning of the case you will answer today.'

Bracewell sat back. 'I have to object,' he said. 'That rather vague letter, which we have read, does not lay out grounds for a case against my client. Therefore he has not been given the information to fairly prepare for this hearing.'

'In my experience, the best way to sort this out,' Kraver said, in a low voice, 'is that we follow the process, so this doesn't turn into a Mad Hatter's Tea Party. So it's best you listen first, speak second.'

'You will have,' O'Donnell said, addressing Bracewell with a shrill voice, 'the chance to speak. But I believe it only fair that we present the case towards your client before we progress further.'

'There's a few items on here,' Robertson continued. 'All of which I know Paul has raised during various meetings with you, Mr. Pendleton.'

'Oh, yes. Many times,' Kraver said.

'Firstly, the charge that you misinformed a parent that their child was sick, on the 7th June last year, when they were not. Thereby causing undue stress and concern to a parent.'

'I can barely remember,' I said. 'But if that is referring to Jordan Slade...'

'Confidentiality, Ben,' Kraver said, flashing a smile. 'There is such a thing as confidentiality.' He looked at the panel, garnering sympathy, before rubbing his chin. 'But what I find strange here, is that you don't even recall this incident. Do you often struggle with your memory?'

'I'm not sure what you mean.'

'Interesting,' Kraver said.

'This brings us onto the second point,' Robertson said, sliding glasses onto his nose. 'It has been noted, by Mr. Kraver, that you made a number of errors in administration during the course of your record keeping.'

'This has been a time of great stress. As you know,' I said, looking hard at Kraver, 'my daughter passed away not so long ago. When I get the chance to speak I will be very keen to talk about how all of this stems from that.'

'So, for the record, you are claiming that the stress of your bereavement is an excuse for lapses in your professionalism?'

'Not at all,' I said. 'I am saying that following her death, I tried to instigate an enquiry from this school, and all of a sudden...'

'Mr. Pendleton,' Robertson snapped, pulling off his glasses. 'Now, we have agreed that in this meeting you will answer each point in turn. In the interests of clarity?'

'I have no recollection of being told I was making errors in my administration. Beyond that which may be considered normal. I'd like to add, they are being brought up now–'

'Thank you, Mr. Pendleton, that is the response which I required.'

I shot a look at Bracewell.

'We all know,' Kraver said, leaning forward and balancing the tips of his fingers together, 'that bereavement can be tough. But I have to mention to the panel, at this point, that since his bereavement, Mr. Pendleton has often been very argumentative.'

'Argumentative?'

'Okay, let's say "aggressive",' Kraver said. I leant back. 'Surely you'd concede, Mr. Pendleton, that being aggressive does not help us to get a positive energy flowing round here?'

'I think if your daughter died, and you knew that you were being attacked, you would be more than–'

'Mr. Pendleton,' Robertson said. 'The charges you are levelling at Mr. Kraver, who is merely following due process, are extremely contentious. Can I suggest that you just offer a balanced response to each point on this agenda, rather than giving us even *more* charges to level against you? Trust me, you've more than enough on your plate as it is.'

Bracewell nodded. I put my head down.

'Thank you. The next charge is that by not taking a sufficient number of breaks during your working hours you endangered the welfare of the pupils.'

'I endangered the welfare of the students? I'm sorry, but that is preposterous.'

Kraver touched his nose. 'So you are saying you believe it's preposterous for us to require that a teacher takes regular breaks? But how else can they stay at their best? In any walk of life, if you're a bricklayer or a rocket scientist, you have to sometimes press pause to collect yourself. Then, you get on with your day, once your mind is fresh again.'

I shook my head. 'At times we are all over-stretched. We try to deal with the workload we have in front of us. If I have ever worked through breaks, it has only ever been in the interests of student welfare.'

'Note that down,' Kraver said. 'Mr. Pendleton believes that these lapses in judgement are actually in the *interests* of the student welfare.'

'Done?' Robertson asked. 'Now, the last charge is that you took unlicensed sick leave following your bereavement, which Mr. Kraver did not authorize.'

+ + + + +

Without her saying anything, I knew Juliette well enough to know when she had been listening against a door. Judging by the strained, confused looks on their faces when Bracewell and I went outside, she and Phillip had seemingly heard the entire hearing from the hallway. As Robertson and Kraver left the room behind us Phillip stood sharply up, pulling his sleeves over his elbow. The two of them cut quickly past him.

We formed a conspiratorial semi-circle.

'How do you think it went?' Phillip asked, trying to nod his rage into a more thoughtful stance.

'I heard every word,' Juliette said, looking between us. 'They barely let you speak, Ben. They promised at the beginning they would give you the chance, as well. They just said his "thoughts about these enquiries are already on record". I think you should have protested at that point, Simon,' she said.

Bracewell ushered her back into her chair. 'Let's all just sit down and wait for their verdict,' he said.

Juliette banged the back of her head against the wall in frustration. 'And what's this about Ben being offered an assessment review prior to the hearing, to discuss his thoughts about all this? That isn't true, is it Ben?'

'Of course not. I would never have turned down that opportunity,' I said, in a low voice.

'I must admit, that one slipped through the net,' Bracewell said. 'By adding to the minutes of today's meeting that they discussed offering you an assessment review, they are covering their backs. It stops them from looking like bad employers and makes this question about your Fitness to Practice seem part of a long process they've been going through with you. They know full well that they offered you no such review.'

'So they got you to sign the minutes at the end?' Phillip asked.

I nodded.

'But they didn't give you the chance to read them! I'm a bit worried that they might now say you've accepted some of those ridiculous accusations, as a result.'

Juliette slumped back in her chair. 'My concern is that *Phillip* should have gone in there instead of you,' she said, eyeballing Bracewell.

'Christ,' Phillip said. 'You must have done a shit job.'

'He'd have torn them to shreds!' she whispered.

Bracewell pushed a hand through his slick hair. 'The reason I didn't push harder is because they take a dim view of solicitors being present in the first place. Believe me, it would have been worse if I wasn't there.'

'I doubt it,' Juliette whispered. 'Ben was just railroaded into accepting a narrative about him that he knows isn't true. I think you've made the situation worse.'

Phillip leant over Juliette and put a hand on my knee. 'You put up a decent fight at the end there though, mate. You even managed to mention Walker.'

'But I bet that didn't make the minutes,' I said.

Juliette hung her head in her hands. I could see, from the occasional spasm of her body, that she was having to expend all of her will to refrain from crying.

I had never felt so neutered, but so enraged. I felt my fists squeezing together, blood blooming in my temples. Where was Marine in all this? Swamped by false paperwork, out of reach.

Phillip put a hand on my shoulder. 'With any luck, they'll see you're not going down without a fight, and they'll let this blow over,' he said.

At that moment Robertson appeared at the top of the stairway.

'What's the news?' Juliette croaked, getting to her feet.

'This is most unprecedented,' Robertson said. 'And not the news you are perhaps hoping for. W-w-w-w.'

We all stood, waiting for his stammer to pass. 'W-w-w.'

'For *Christ's sake*,' Phillip said. 'Is this really how the school is run? Kraver's sent you to do his dirty work. Donkeys sent by donkeys.'

Robertson looked at the floor. 'The panel didn't get the chance to reach a decision, as Paul Kraver stated that he was not prepared to supervise you anymore. As such, that forces this case from being informal to being formal. You will now have to answer *formal* claims about your Fitness to Practice, in another hearing.'

'Jesus,' Phillip said. 'Kraver is just forcing you into a situation where he can make false charges against you official. He's already got those minutes signed, so he can pretend you've accepted these bullshit accusations.' He addressed Robertson, directly. 'Do you realize that you're part of a character assassination?' he hissed. Robertson didn't reply. 'Course not. You look like you wouldn't run if your arse was on fire. This is a kangaroo court!'

Robertson looked at the floor. 'Sometimes,' he said, 'the process has flaws. There is n-n-n-nothing I can do. You will get the chance to make your voice heard at the formal hearing, which will happen as soon as possible. I suggest you just allow this process to take its course.'

When he had gone, with everyone looking up at the ceiling, Phillip leant towards me again. 'We have to get you on TV before this formal hearing,' he said. 'You have to save your reputation before they officially ruin it.'

'I just hope they don't get wind of you going on television in the next three days,' Bracewell whispered. 'Because if they do, you can bet they will schedule the formal hearing the morning before the show. So that by the time you try and fight your corner, you are *already* banned from teaching.'

Phillip stood up. 'Presumably your appearance will be in the TV listings, so they will hear about it coming up?'

'Three days is too soon for even Kraver to put together a formal hearing. Unless he has planned this all along to ensure you are formally charged of something in the next day or two.'

'I hadn't thought of that,' I said.

'So we can't get you in front of the cameras quick enough,' Juliette said.

At the thought of being on the television, I was bitterly disappointed to again feel something rise in my throat. I tore from my chair and into the gents toilets. The hot fluid scalded my mouth as it passed into the bowl. As I tried to steady myself against the wall I heard Bracewell, from outside. 'You all have to have faith,' he was saying. 'These systems exist for a reason. They keep our country what it is.'

I sat down, and as I took deep breaths I heard Juliette trying to calm Phillip down.

'No, Juliette. I'm not going to listen to this jingoistic rubbish,' he was saying.

'It's not rubbish,' Bracewell responded. 'Our constitution has existed for hundreds of years, and it survives because it works.'

'It doesn't work,' Phillip fumed. 'If it did, Ben wouldn't be in this situation, don't you see?'

I couldn't hear Bracewell's response, but Phillip's riposte was loud enough.

'Don't talk to me about the Dunkirk spirit,' Phillip said. 'Even if it got us through a war, it didn't manage to survive until now. This is a nation of people watching their own back, and their bank balance. Nothing more. You think Jimmy Savile would have got away with it if it was anything else? No one wanted to speak out because they didn't want to risk anything, and all the large institutions that we're told to adore just let it happen. You have any idea how many people must have known about that scandal, who could have stopped it? How many people were complicit, with their silence? That situation just needed one hero, in the right place, and it never came.'

'It's true. Ben can be that man,' Juliette said. 'You two don't know him like I do.' There was a strength to her tone. 'At the beginning of our relationship he showed strength that I've never known in anyone else. He can do it.'

I stood upright, and moved over to the mirror. I didn't recognize my reflection. He seemed altered somehow, almost to the point of being a different man. I wondered if Juliette was right about him. Our enemies shape us as much as our friends, I thought.

NINETEEN

'I WOULDN'T TAKE too much notice of Phillip's cynicism,' Violet said, biting her bottom lip as she plunged the percolator.

'I take him with a pinch of salt,' I answered. 'But I've found there's always truth in what he says. So, you think you've got the measure of him?'

'I take him with a pinch of salt too. I've got my faults,' Violet said, as the percolator splashed coffee onto her wrists. 'Being incredibly clumsy is evidently just one of them.'

She moved her hand over the sink and doused it under the cold jet. I took in for a moment the long, somehow unsure curve of her body, the hair lapped over each shoulder. 'But being a poor judge of character isn't.'

'I should take that as a compliment, then,' I said.

Phillip had spent the afternoon, with Art, vigorously schooling me in preparation for the TV interview. Under pressure from Phillip, Art had confirmed that filming would definitely take place the following day. I imagined Juliette had spent the afternoon loitering around at home, waiting for the letter about the formal hearing to arrive.

As Art and Phillip traded notes in the living room, Violet poured us both a strong, black coffee in the kitchen. It had been a shock and a guilty pleasure to see her at Phillip's house on arrival. Noticing my reaction, she had quickly insisted that she was 'just here to see how you're getting on'.

I felt acutely aware of my responsibility to manage the situation with her. To not get any closer to her, but at the same time to not look reticent.

'Does Phillip know about what happened with us?' she whispered.

'No. I really think he was hoping something would happen with the two of you. So he can't know about us.'

'I see,' she said. 'So now I'm your dirty secret?'

'No. That's not it at all.'

'Did you say anything to Juliette?' Something in her eyes betrayed that Violet had been considering the question deeply.

'It's not the right time,' I said.

'When do you think the right time might be?'

I tried to weigh up her tone. I found myself checking where Phillip and Art were. Phillip was showing off the functions of his new wide-screen TV, and telling him how it was great for watching porn on. Violet heard the puerile exchange, and smiled.

'See why I'm perhaps more interested in you?'

'I'm caught between a rock and a hard place here, Violet. If I do tell Juliette what happened she'll want to hear that it meant nothing and was a silly accident. But the problem is…'

Violet sucked on her scalded wrist. 'It did mean something?' she said.

'How did you know?' I asked.

'A lucky guess. Of course, there's no way I feel exactly the same,' she said, with a sarcastic smile.

I smiled back, considering her expression.

'So how was the media training?' she asked, leaning against the work surface.

'They seem to think I can suddenly turn into this evangelical preacher man, in front of a live studio audience, while I happen to be sweating buckets,' I said, taking the cup of coffee from her.

'Don't worry about all that stuff about your posture and that. That'll just make you overthink it.' She dropped her voice, as she moved towards me. Her scent was as enticing as before. But this time it reassured as much as it seduced. 'You know what I first liked about you, when I saw "Educating Bristol"?' she asked.

I had a sudden flash of memory. Violet, her mouth open with pleasure, as we writhed together on her sheets. I pushed it from my mind.

'No.'

'That you weren't self-conscious at all. That you had no ego. When I watched you on that show, it wasn't that charismatic speech in the after-school detention that I liked. It was the fact that when you were in front of those children you were entirely at their service. You'd have mooed like a cow, brayed like a donkey, or swung from the chandeliers to give them the information you wanted them to have.'

'Swung from the chandeliers?'

'Okay, perhaps not that. But what I'm saying is, when you're on TV, I think you should think of the whole country like one massive classroom.'

A stray lock of her hair fell onto her cheeks. I remembered the sky blue hair band she pulled from her hair as she straddled me on her bed.

'You don't believe me, do you?' she said. 'If you can tame a room of Year Elevens and get them through their GCSEs, you can tame one fattening presenter and a load of armchair critics. You'll be mint.'

I took a sip of coffee, and gazed through the doorway. Art was gathering up papers.

'You know,' I said. 'I think that might be the only sensible advice I've had all day.'

'You're welcome.'

'Thanks,' I said. 'Thanks for… being supportive. Given our whole situation.'

'It'll blow over. I'll still be here,' she said.

I took a sip. 'Right,' I said.

TWENTY

AS PHILLIP and I gave our names at the BBC reception I tried to take in the surroundings. Lurid, pop-art portraits of famous comedians mocked us from on high. The muted buzz of private correspondence leaked out from the glass-walled offices around us. All this, I told myself, was machinery of a new kind. Carefully built to coax entertainment, from a select few, out for the masses. Yet here I was, about to use all this machinery to express something far darker.

Phillip knowingly conducted a hushed exchange with a red-haired receptionist. Formalities dealt with, she moved from behind her desk to reveal a striking dress decorated in neon chevrons. She offered coffee and ushered us through to the studio, where passes were flashed at a silent, surly guard.

I reminded myself of the whole point of this journey. The moment would come, in a few hours, when I would have to ignore all the pressure to provide entertainment, to simply say what I needed to say. I dreaded the thought of it, and found my fists clenching, in a vain effort to relax my arms.

We were told to wait on a sofa in the open-plan lounge inside the studio. Runners flitted about us, pressing earpieces hard into their heads. Phillip's leg began to twitch. 'I can see this is asking a lot of you,' he said, turning to me. 'I've done two of these interviews and I still don't understand how they work.'

'How did they go?' I asked.

He exhaled, dramatically. 'The first time my flies were undone, and in the playback you could make out a tiny knot of red throughout the whole chat.'

'Your boxer shorts?'

He did a double take at me. 'Of course it was my boxer shorts,' he said.

'Yeah, yeah,' I agreed.

'And the second time I told an anecdote about a mad priest at my school, who was caught flashing these schoolgirls on the number 39 bus one afternoon. No one laughed. When I raised this with the host afterwards he told me that the first two rows of the audience had been made up of priests in training, on a field trip.'

A blonde woman in a pleated skirt, jittering with nervous energy arrived moments later. She was clutching a clipboard. 'We'll take you to makeup,' she said. 'We're running a little behind schedule, so I'll have to brief you whilst they get you ready.'

'Makeup?' I said. 'Is that really necessary?'

'Trust me mate, when the lights are on you, there'll be one hell of a shine on that spam of a forehead you have,' Phillip said. The blonde lady laughed, the stud in her nose catching the light.

'My advice would be to keep your jacket on too,' Phillip said, as we stood up. 'Those lights don't half make you sweat.'

As I was dabbed with makeup, on a high stool in front of a mirror framed with naked bulbs, a lady with a shock of pink hair rattled through Peterson's questions. 'He'll want to talk a lot about that girl Aaliyah, and why you care about the welfare of children,' she started.

Phillip peered over a copy of The Daily Mirror, from his chair nearby.

'*Why I care,*' I whispered, after she'd gone.

'Caring seems to have become a rare commodity,' Phillip said. 'Even pretending to care is becoming one too. Now, remember. Peterson is being paid a lot of money to coax an entertaining interview out of you, and he already likes you. He'll just be relieved that you want to talk.' He waited until a runner had passed him by. 'You just make damn sure you use this chance,' he said. 'This is your one crack at telling the world about what happened with Marine.'

I could feel my phone buzzing in my pocket. I reached down for it. My inbox was full of new messages from Juliette.

All of them seemed to start with the word 'Remember'.

Flicking through, I noticed that they were studded with one or two from Violet. I can't handle this now, I thought.

'It's time,' said the assistant with the nose ring. 'Come on, hurry.'

We were told to wait in the wings. Phillip and I watched through a break in the thick, red curtain whilst technical assistants straightened leads on the studio floor and rushed to consult with one another. I could hear a comedian warming up the audience, who were gradually finding their seats, and laying down coats. Small cones of light denoted people furtively turning off phones. The comic was riffing about how his fiancé was withholding food from him, forcing him to diet with her as their wedding approached. 'I'm happy to lose weight if she is,' he was saying to them. 'But how far does it go? Do I need to wear a dress on the day too, so she doesn't feel alone with that?'

'Christ, he is awful,' Phillip said. 'That barely even makes sense.'

The sheer size of the audience only became apparent, as their titters of amusement became waves of laughter. Phillip poked his head through the curtain. 'Blimey,' he said. 'It's a full house.'

'I've never dealt with a class this big,' I said, thinking of Violet's advice.

'What are you on about?' he asked.

I tried to recall Violet's words. They had soothed me at the time, but how would I teach a room full of students about a scandal? Step by step, I thought. Making sure that every stage had been absorbed before I moved onto the next.

The audience roared with laughter, and at the same instant I felt sweat bloom in my arm pits. I buttoned up my jacket. I felt my forehead, already slick. I gulped, and prayed that I wouldn't be sick, and have to rush off stage halfway through the interview. How would I manage?

The comedian bounded offstage, rubbing his temples as he joined us in the wings. The Floor Manager walked through the curtain. 'We've got one hell of a line up for you ladies and gentlemen,' he said, pacing awkwardly in front of the crowd as he read off an iPad. 'Fresh off a flight from The Congo, everyone's favorite heartthrob explorer–'

'That's not you,' Phillip said.

'Peter Jefferson!' he announced.

The audience cheered.

'We've got interviews with Ben Pendleton, star of "Educating Bristol", and music from a smashing new Manchester electro-pop band, Scythe. Live, here, tonight!'

'Now ignore all that,' Phillip whispered, leaning into me. 'He'll want a few fun anecdotes about life at the school to kick-off. Remember that one we talked about, when the school was snowed in and–'

'And the Shakespearean actors had to perform in the playground.'

'You can always wheel that out, if you really need it.'

'Yeah, it's a real humdinger,' I said, shaking my head.

'She said they'd cut to some footage from the show and then Marine will be mentioned. Then you just ease your way into the story. But you'll need to get the audience onside straight away, okay?'

'I'll do my best,' I said.

'And lastly,' the announcer was saying, his words booming around the auditorium, 'we will have a short set from the woman who is bringing clowning back to 21st century audiences. Andrea Myers!'

'Phillip?'

He was trying to peek through the curtains again.

'What?'

'You know - thanks.'

He didn't look at me.

'Don't be daft,' he said. 'Why wouldn't I help you?'

'I don't know.'

The announcer's voice blasted out, louder than ever.

'Now can you please all give a big warm welcome to your host. Craig Peterson!'

+ + + + +

I stood rooted to the spot, trying through the crack in the curtain to follow the repartee between Peterson and his guests. The conversations fizzled past me, a stream of postmodern noise that I couldn't understand. They talked about pop stars I'd never heard of, celebrity workouts, programmes I didn't know existed. I racked my brains for anecdotes on each subject, and found nothing.

My name was announced. A stagehand took me by the crook of my elbow.

'You'll be brilliant,' Phillip said, as the curtains opened, letting in a flood of light. 'Just remember to smile.'

The lights blinded me. A roar from the crowd went up. As I stumbled out from the curtain the glare began to sting my eyes. I moved onto the stage and as I turned to the audience each person was a blurred silhouette.

Peterson took my hand and guided me across a shiny, black floor on which a white sofa beckoned. Peterson sat in a leather armchair opposite me as the din subsided.

His skin was bright and clear, his eyes an unsettling shade of blue. As I settled into the sofa he smiled at me. His sleekness evoked a greyhound.

'Ben, it's great to have you on the show,' he said, his voice smooth. 'I loved "Educating Bristol", my wife and I are simply avid fans. But the first question I have to ask you is this. What did your missus make of that nurse's outfit?'

The audience burst into laughter.

For a moment I was stumped. Which outfit did he mean?

'The n-nurse's outfit, you mean?' I asked.

'You know, when you got that student those seven GCSEs. And you agreed to appear at assembly dressed as a nurse. Right?'

'Oh, of course.'

'I'm glad my teachers were a bit quicker off the mark than you!' he said.

The audience laughed again. A hollow sound, that rattled in my insides.

'Yeah, I've kept that outfit in storage,' I said. 'You never know when a student might need that extra push - so I'm not throwing it away just yet.'

Some titters.

'Great stuff,' he said, crossing his legs. 'Now, I watched the show, and I was genuinely impressed by your teaching, Ben. When I was at school my English teacher Mrs. Robinson said I'd never be a high flier, Ben, and it hurt me. It hurt me.'

He clasped his hands to his chest to illustrate the pain.

'Yeah, well. Look at you now,' I said.

'Yeah, and look at her. Well you can't, she's dead.'

The audience roared.

'Could be worse,' I said. 'She could be on a zero hours contract.'

The audience kept laughing.

'I like it,' he said. 'Topical. And people say teachers can't be hip. Isn't that unfair, Ben?'

'Deeply wrong,' I said, nodding.

'Now tell me, Ben,' he continued, folding his legs. 'What is it really like being a teacher these days? Because you can't be strict anymore, can you? And let's face it, some parents will drop off kids that are right thickies.'

'It depends on the student,' I said. 'Marie, who you mentioned, was exceptional. One day during an afternoon detention, out of nowhere, she suddenly gave me this tremendous speech.' I sat up straight. 'And it moved me, you know? So I made this silly promise about wearing that outfit if she succeeded and I think that suddenly brought her mission to life. From then on, her goal wasn't just a private thing for her to slave over on her own. It became an event for everyone to talk about.' He was nodding. 'I knew the more she talked about getting me in that nurse's outfit,' I continued, 'the more clearly she could imagine achieving her goal.'

'Brilliant,' Peterson said, 'absolutely brilliant. Now, let's show the audience a clip.'

He turned to a screen above our heads, which I hadn't noticed amongst the fake city scape behind us. I twitched as a reel of my 'best of moments'- none of which I found particularly funny – were screened. The audience seemed to enjoy it.

How can we get from here to Marine, I wondered? Behind Peterson, in the wings, I could see Phillip giving me a thumbs up.

'Great stuff,' Peterson said, turning back to me as the sound faded. 'But it hasn't always been happy times, has it, Ben? I understand that shortly after that series ended you and your family suffered a great loss?'

I looked down, shocked by the sudden gear change. 'Yes. A few months after that series wrapped our beloved daughter, Marine, lost her life on a school trip.'

The audience gave a collective sob. I felt as if I was in a pantomime. This is it, I thought. It has to happen now.

'And the verdict was that it was an accident? A terrible accident, that's every parent's worst nightmare.'

I could feel the importance of the moment. The camera was there, beaming into every home. The audience were listening. Phillip was poised, expectant.

'It was a nightmare, Craig, and to be honest we haven't woken up from it. I think the main barrier to recovery has been learning that perhaps it wasn't simply an accident.'

In the wings I could see Phillip stand up straight, his hand on his chin. The audience had fallen silent. Even Peterson, the consummate professional, seemed surprised by how sharply the tone had changed.

'Okay. Can you tell us more?'

I nodded.

'Marine was on a field trip, walking along the local moor with the rest of her class,' I said, weighing my words. 'We got a call to say that there had been an accident and when we got to the scene we learnt that Marine had taken a serious fall. Shortly after, she lost the battle for her life. She died on that field trip.'

The words rang out, louder than I had expected. My collar felt tight. I felt the heat of the scorching lights. I wondered what those silent silhouettes in the audience were thinking. I looked over at Phillip. He gestured, frantically, that I should go on.

'I see,' Peterson said, nodding.

'The member of staff supposed to be looking after Marine at the time said that she broke away from the pack and fell off the cliff edge before he could recover her. But we later heard that he had been previously been found guilty of offences towards young girls. Naturally, we started to question the official account we'd been given of what happened.'

Peterson nodded. I wondered if I could sense panic in his eyes. In the wings Phillip nodded harder. Push on, I told myself. Don't stop now, that wasn't enough.

'I asked the school to look into this allegation during their enquiry. To find out if this temporary member of staff really had been guilty of such crimes in the past. And if so, why had he been employed by the school?'

'And what did you find out?' Peterson asked, carefully.

'We found out that this man had got CRB clearance under a new name, and that once he had a job at the school he was assigned to the school trip. I have also been told that the school's headmaster was informed of his past, but still continued to employ him.'

Peterson looked at the camera. 'And I suppose that we must stress, at this stage, that this is all alleged.'

'Yes. And it remains only alleged, until it is properly investigated.

The big question for us is - what exactly happened to take my daughter so close to the cliff edge in the first place?'

'And so the implication here is that it wasn't an accident, she was trying to get away from this man?' Peterson slowly weaved his fingers together. I suddenly had the feeling that I was engaged in a game of chess with him now as well.

'Exactly,' I said. 'At this stage it is only a rumour. But what caused even more devastation to my partner and me was the fact that the school did not properly investigate this claim at all. Their enquiry was a whitewash, and they did not even interview the people that I had been assured they would speak to. When I pushed for there to be a proper investigation, suddenly I found myself facing questions about my own Fitness to Practice.'

I could see, behind Peterson's eyes, his brain whirring. 'And you can prove that there were never any questions about your fitness before you had called their professionalism into question?'

'Indeed. Not only that, Craig, but since they suspended me, I have heard about various other people who've had similar experiences. Having raised a question against an officiating body they too have seen themselves suddenly being scrutinized.'

'A case of tarnish the troublemaker to save their own skin?'

'Exactly. In fact, soon I am having to attend a Formal Fitness to Practice hearing to face what are clearly trumped up charges devised by Paul Kraver, the headmaster of the school.'

At the mention of Kraver I saw Phillip punch the air. I tried to suppress a smile, as Phillip ground one fist into an open hand.

'And I understand that your partner, Juliette, has organized online a petition about this,' Peterson said, glancing at the autocue. 'It's entitled "Justice for the Pendleton Family".'

This was news to me.

'You look surprised, Ben, but it seems your better half has

come out fighting here. This petition is online, people, at www. change.org, and it lobbies for the Attorney General to apply to the High Court for a new inquest to be held into Marine's death. It also lobbies for the Education Secretary to intervene, and have the Fitness to Practice case against you dropped. For there to instead be an investigation into the headmaster who's allowed this to happen under his watch.'

I opened my mouth to speak, but could not. Juliette had organized this? I had seen so little of her since the fight had begun, that I *had* wondered what she'd been up to. I felt a snag in my heart. I had got close to Violet, thinking that she wasn't there for me. But she had been planning this all along. As I looked up, a screen grab of the online petition was being shown overhead.

'As you can see, at the moment the petition only has fourteen signatures.' Peterson turned to the audience. 'Can I take it we will all be adding our names to it tonight?'

The audience roared a resounding 'yes'.

I felt a spasm of relief, a bolt of sheer happiness shooting through me. Peterson leant forward, and the feel of his hand on my shoulder made me bow my head. The audience gave out a loud cry of sympathy. I knew then that Juliette had planned this to be a surprise, knowing it would be the only way for me to look emotionally overwhelmed at exactly the right moment, for us to get the public onboard.

'I appreciate this must be difficult for you,' Peterson said. 'But the fight back has now begun.' He turned to the audience. 'Hasn't it?' he said to them.

Their spirited response was almost too much to take. I looked up and smiled at them, and as I did I saw a few of the rows of silhouettes get to their feet and applaud. I could see the faces of mothers, fathers, young students. Earrings, haircuts, trembling smiles. Their expressions exquisite portraits of sympathy, and anger. Smiling, and clapping me.

'I think we should cut to a break,' Peterson said.

TWENTY-ONE

I SAT AT THE BACK of the café, unable to sit still. It wasn't just the energy of the young staff, as they darted to and fro, that unsettled me. It was the thought of Violet arriving at any moment. As I saw her open the door, smiling from under a pink alice band, I felt a sudden swoop in my stomach.

With mitten-covered hands she gesticulated to the waiter, ordering us two cups of coffee. I was suddenly conscious of my suit jacket, slightly frayed, and the open necked collar which marked me out from the lurid t-shirts around us. Lithe bodies relaxed into expansive sofas, as their hands tapped at chrome laptops.

'Congratulations, Ben,' she said, kissing my cheek. 'I saw the interview. You were so good.'

'Thanks,' I said. 'I'm hoping it was the start of something,' I said.

She began to unwrap herself, like an elaborately decorated chocolate. I tried to focus on the menu as she settled into the chair opposite me.

Her eyes dissected me, darting between my face and the menu I was holding with a look of suppressed amusement. I was sure she knew I was just pretending to study it, to try and conceal her effect on me. I wondered if she knew how much power she had over me. Over my relationship with Phillip and my family. How had I handed so much of my livelihood over to someone I barely knew, in one night?

'I just read online that the petition has gained over half a million signatures,' she said. 'There's articles in The Times, The Express, from all over the world. The coroner is going to have to tell the police to reopen the enquiry about Marine now. It's clearly a matter of public interest.'

'I don't think it's the public interest that will force her to open it up again,' I said, smiling at a waitress with pink candyfloss hair. She placed the steaming coffees in front of us, small wisps of heat oozing from the foamy surfaces. I waited until she'd departed, wiping her hands on her apron.

'Bracewell says the reason the coroner will reopen the case is because new evidence has come to light,' I said.

'You found evidence that they're attacking you?'

Her question seemed almost defensive. I weighed up the way it had been made, decided to think nothing of it.

'I didn't find evidence, no. It was Marine's teacher, Katy. On the school trip she was a little disturbed by Walker, and in the aftermath of it I told her about Kraver forcing me to take leave. I think she got the sense that something was being hidden. She doesn't seem the bold type, but she must be. She started to surreptitiously do some digging, using what she knew about Walker's past. Eventually she found a photograph from his school yearbook. Except that in it he isn't David Walker, he's called "Toby Young".'

'So he changed his name. So what?'

'She also found a clipping from his local Gazette, which has a picture of a teacher, called Toby Young, above an article about how he was found guilty of sexually abusing a young girl in his class. My guess is that there are more cases we don't know about.'

'How on earth did he get past the Criminal Records check to work at your school then?'

'Perhaps the school didn't do its homework, and he just slipped through the net. Or perhaps there's a little more to it?'

She blinked hard, processing the input. 'It can't be that easy to get CRB clearance after you've changed your name.'

I sipped. 'I looked into it. The guidelines state that the school must see the "appropriate paperwork from the applicant" before they can support a name change.'

She laughed. 'Like you found that out,' she said, stirring the spoon in her cup.

'It wasn't me,' I said. 'It was Juliette.'

Violet blanched at my mention of a name which we had studiously avoided using. 'Course it was,' she said. 'So I can only assume this Walker fella didn't have paperwork to support his application? Otherwise they'd have been able to find out about his past.'

'Yes. In which case they should have had a discussion with him, about why he wanted to change his name.'

'They must have done a pretty sloppy job.' She curled her hands around her cup.

'Perhaps,' I said. 'But the most powerful bit of evidence Katy found is an email from a member of staff, sent to Kraver, telling him the rumours about Walker. Asking him to investigate them.'

'She's a right little detective, this Katy woman. Does she realize she's risking her job?'

'I think she does, which is why she was hesitant in coming forward at first. She still doesn't want me to blow her cover. I think she feels guilty that she didn't do more on the day Marine fell. I suspect she's been working under the radar to try and stop her conscience needling her.'

'And let me guess, Kraver didn't properly investigate Walker even after his past was flagged up?'

Violet selected some sugar from the pot in front of her, and poured it onto the foam. I watched it float for a while, before invisible seepage broke the surface.

'Well, as Kraver had *already* employed Walker, he knew that investigating him would only cause trouble if something was found. So he just fobbed off the email, and kept Walker at the school.'

'Sounds pretty fishy to me,' she said. 'Surely he could see a few steps ahead and work out that sooner or later he'd be found responsible. So why would he take the risk?'

'I've thought about that. Either it was arrogance, or perhaps Kraver can't afford not to cover for Walker. I'm wondering if perhaps Walker has something on him.'

'I'm sure you mentioned to me that he was very suddenly brought in as a headmaster? And that he's already made a lot of unusual decisions?'

'That's right, yeah. For one, it's rare for a headmaster to come in with a background in media, rather than teaching. There's this new campus opening soon, and with this recent government move to privatize more education I think he was brought in to help develop the school as a franchise. A money-making venture.'

'Sounds like he has friends in high places, otherwise he wouldn't have been appointed at all. So then perhaps he has to take on members of staff that he *doesn't* want to take on. Perhaps he has to be seen to defend decisions that privately he wouldn't stand by? It happens more and more when commerce comes into the public services. In which case, Ben, you're going to need to be conscious of the fact that he could have support from some pretty powerful people.'

I nodded. 'So this next hearing could be a case of "strong force meets immovable object."'

She liked the analogy. 'Still, you've got a few surprises up your sleeve now thanks to this Katy, haven't you?'

'I hope they will be surprises,' I said, 'but I can't help wishing the next few days would just pass so I can get it over with. Bracewell is sure the Education Secretary will have to intervene now he's been lobbied so powerfully by Juliette's petition. I'm hoping that he will, and he'll say the hearing should get cancelled.'

'I'm sorry, Ben, but I don't think that's going to happen.' She looked at my hand, then moved to hold it, before restraining herself. 'If he did that the Education Secretary would be seriously undermining the school. I know it will be tough, but you're going to have to face up to it. Can you do that?'

I nodded, once, but on the second nod was unable to move my head. My jaw locked. When she smiled, in sympathy, I cracked and pushed my hands through my hair. 'Oh God,' I said. 'First the TV interview, now this. This is going to be so much worse, isn't it? Because in *this* hearing Kraver is going to go all out to damage my name. If a formal panel find me guilty of something, that will stay on my record permanently. No one will employ me for the rest of my life.'

Violet winced. As she did sunlight from outside streamed through her hair, illuminating its tips. 'I'm not going to lie to you, Ben, it probably will be dead tricky. But you have the people on your side now. And you need to be charismatic enough to channel their energy. Which of course you can be.'

She smiled, and I felt a tingle of pleasure in my jaw.

'What do you mean?' I gulped at the cooling coffee.

'Well, you need to find a way to be the focal point for the anger of all those people. So that when you stand up there it's not Ben versus Kraver, its every single person who's backed you versus him.'

'And how exactly do I do that? I'm a teacher, not Martin Luther King!'

'Well, if you want to get *back* to teaching it looks like you'll need to be a bit *like* Martin Luther King. Have you ever watched Prime Minister's Questions?'

I nodded. 'They just tend to shout at each other though, don't they?'

She smiled. 'True, but there is more to it than that. You ever notice who comes out on top? During the days of Blair and Cameron, it was always the person who channelled the cheers of their supporters who came out on top. The person with the glint in their eye, who looks like they love the thrill of the fight. That glint may well be artificial, Ben, but you avoid tapping into the power of your supporters at your own peril.'

'This Kraver is pretty overpowering. He has the knack of giving his opinions like their facts, and people seem to just let him.'

'Then it is even more important that you do what I'm saying.'

'So what do I do, print out all the tweets that have been written about me and distribute them at the door?'

She laughed. 'You can't print tweets out, Ben. You're not exactly Mr. Current Affairs, are you? You *should* look online and see what people are saying about your case, though. I think you'd be pleasantly surprised.'

She took her laptop out of her rucksack, placed it on the table, and opened the shiny slab. Violet squinted behind me, at a wall where I noticed a Wi-Fi password was scrawled, in green chalk.

'I will,' I said. 'Because if this hearing ends with Kraver winning, and me getting banned from teaching, I won't be able to raise the money to pay Bracewell's bills. Our life will be over, in so many ways. Right now it does feel a bit like everyone is putting more and more chips on the table, and it all depends on what happens at this one hearing. And judging from what happened at the last one, I know Kraver will play dirty.'

'He'll be planning other ways to attack you too,' she said, not meeting my eye. 'You mark my words. He has the backing of quite a complex organisation behind him, and the fight will happen on his turf. Kraver is designing the whole battleground on which this conflict takes place. The setting, the language used in its administration - everything.'

'Well that's why I'm worried.' I said. 'In the last hearing, Kraver got to decide who was on the panel, how long they spoke, and even what made it onto the minutes. This hearing is *formal*, so he'll have even more weapons to bring out.'

'You think he can pick the panel?' she asked, leaning forward and cupping her face in her hands. The light caught her eyes, and their distinct colour engaged me for a moment too long. I focused myself.

'Well, officially, Kraver doesn't get to choose who's on the panel,' I said. 'It has to be a mix of teachers and non-teachers.'

'So, if it becomes apparent that Kraver has planted someone on the panel to do his dirty work, you and Bracewell need to notice that and fight against it. I think you need to change the terms of the enquiry and turn the spotlight back onto Kraver. Let him see how he likes a taste of his own medicine.' She leant closer to the laptop and started typing. 'Now, let me show you what they're saying online.'

'Before you do,' I said, 'how exactly do you think I can give him a taste of his own medicine?'

'You've got to get Bracewell to ask the education authority for the enquiry to be held in public, for a start,' she said. 'Argue it is clearly in the public interest. Harness the support of the people to help you do that. Get them to tweet, petition, whatever. Also, you need to get this Katy to be at the meeting so she can offer her evidence. Along with anyone else who can offer the panel some insights into what Kraver is really like.'

'I think Katy will draw the line there. This secretary at the school, Lorraine Hannerty, apparently spoke to Juliette about how Kraver forced her to relocate onto a different campus when all this blew up. She was the person who initially warned me about Walker, on the day of the fall.'

'She'd love her day in the sun then, wouldn't she?' Violet said.

'And risk getting the sack?'

'You'll have to convince them, Ben. Unless they want Walker, Young - or whatever he calls himself now - to keep doing what he's doing. Anyway, come round here and look at this.'

I tried to ignore the scent of her perfume as I moved round to where Violet was sitting. I took in the bewildering array of symbols on the blue screen. At the top of the screen was the word 'Twitter'. Underneath, text messages vied for attention. I could see, again and again, that each one ended with '#benpendleton'.

'I don't know about social media,' I said.

'But you have got a Facebook account?'

'Why would I have a Facebook account when I've got a family?'

She laughed. 'Social media helped you get your profile in the first place,' she said. 'All the tweets and retweets on here played a big part in your petition getting signed by so many.'

'Tweets?'

'Yeah. Like little posts. Look.'

I took in the messages:

#benpendleton is a hero, speaking the truth to power.

Unfortunately, he's also paved the way for future trials by media.

#benpendleton daughter victim of assault attempt? You try watching #educatingbristol all the way through. That was an assault on my ears!

'You get a few pricks on here,' Violet said. 'It's a bit of a case of "bring out your dead". Democracy at its finest.'

'A lot of this is young people. Shouldn't they be outside, trying to get off with each other or something?'

'Sometimes you don't sound like a teacher.'

I read some more:

#benpendleton is a pioneer. The guy proves that despite the cover-ups of the previous generation, social media gives them nowhere to hide. #truthisamatteroftime

'Check out this one,' Violet said.

Bravo Pendleton for standing up to the man #benpendleton

'It's had 4500 retweets, that one.' She took in my baffled expression. 'So, 4500 people have shared it, Ben.'

'And three thousand said it's their "favourite". But they don't even know me!'

'You're public property now, Ben. There's memes, too. Did you know that?'

She clicked a few times, before pulling up a photo of me, standing in front of a whiteboard on which someone had edited an anarchy symbol. A beard and beret had been added to my head. The picture was captioned 'Che Pendleton'.

'Jesus,' I said.

She laughed. 'Fetching, isn't it? Better than that nurse's uniform. Looks like you've started something. You've proven that online fame is power. Do you have any idea what a splash it would make if you started tweeting about this directly?'

'You think so?'

'I'm setting up an account for you. You can thank these people personally that way, and make statements of your own.'

'Okay. Mind you, Phillip doesn't use the internet much either, and he doesn't seem to be doing too badly. In fact, that reminds me. I'm planning something for him.'

She closed her laptop. 'What, to say thank you? What do you get the man who has everything?'

I leant forward. 'Phillip wouldn't admit this, but he's not been the same since his relationship with Christine ended. Problem is, he doesn't know how to get back in touch with her. So I'm going to make the first step. On his behalf.'

'Ben Pendleton,' she said. 'Teacher, revolutionary, cupid.'

I felt myself blush. 'Give over,' I said.

TWENTY-TWO

THE NIGHT BEFORE the hearing our home was overrun for the
first time since Marine died. Having dispensed her advice, Violet
decided she had to go to a conference that night, and decided to
make herself scarce. But I could not deny, even to myself, that I
had taken her advice completely on board, by sending a message
round and organising a little resistance committee at our home,
to prepare.

Bracewell had been the first to arrive. Ruddy and windswept,
he laid his suitcase down by the couch next to the TV and, sitting
down, he started to arrange his papers on his lap. Juliette, at the
other end of the sofa, closed her laptop. 'The petition is close to
a million,' she said, stretching her arms out above her head. She
looked over at me, stood by the window. 'I was shaking when I
scrolled through the messages that had been left for you, Ben,' she
said. 'There's some real anger out there about what they've done
to us.'

Art arrived a few minutes later, and he noted the number on
Juliette's screen with an almost regal air. I looked over at him as

he poured himself a whisky from the decanter and sat on the armchair opposite the TV. 'You know what this means, don't you, Simon?' he said, turning to our solicitor.

Simon tested a biro, the sharpness of the movement increasing as no ink came out. 'No, what does it mean?' he asked.

'It means we can now argue this is clearly a public interest case. As a result, we could—'

'Lobby the teaching association to make Ben's hearing a public affair,' I finished, walking into the seating area. Art clicked his fingers, jumping upright with excitement. 'Exactly,' he said.

'That way I could channel all this support,' I said. I thought of Violet's advice. 'I want to do that,' I added, a little too emphatically.

'I can't see why they would want to let us make the hearing public, though,' Bracewell said, polishing his glasses on his sleeve. 'Even if we argue it is in the public interest, why would they consent to having their process, and any possible flaws in it, made open for scrutiny?'

'Fear,' I said, beginning to get a handle on the idea. 'They might permit us out of fear of being ridiculed by the public for another cover-up.'

'In principle you're correct,' Bracewell said, exhaling. 'But in reality, when it comes to injustice, a factor comes into play, which I call "realistic rage". I always measure, on a scale of one to ten, how likely it is that a stranger will bother to take up someone else's cause. I think this case would score about an eight, because parents will be scared at the thought of this happening with their children. So we should try. If the teachers' association were to say yes, and the hearing was to be conducted publicly, it would make it much harder for Kraver to try his usual railroading tactics.'

'Harder, but not impossible,' Phillip answered. He'd seemingly been lingering at our ajar front door.

'Here he is,' I said. 'Your usual?'

He nodded. I moved over to the decanter, and responded to Juliette and Bracewell's wave for a dram. I poured myself a glass. The fuel of the revolution, I thought, smiling at the memory of the Che Guevara meme.

'If I have any sort of role in this motley Rebel Alliance,' Phillip said, moving to the spare armchair close to me, 'it will probably relate to Ben's presentation of himself at this hearing.'

'You did a good job getting him ready for TV,' Art said, raising a glass.

Phillip accepted the tumbler from me, and I placed the others on the glass table before perching on the arm of Juliette's chair. She moved into the kitchen as Phillip nodded to himself. 'I know enough about this Kraver fellow to know that he will have done everything he can to create, on the day, a set-up that works in his favour,' he said.

'He already has,' Art said. 'It's the night before the hearing and Ben still doesn't have a full itinerary of the charges he'll have to answer. They're making sure he's not prepared to properly defend himself. I think the best use of our time this evening will be to put together a list of imagined charges that we think would damage you most, Ben. That is what they'll be planning to do. Then we can prepare to answer them. How one earth Kraver has managed to make sure Ben doesn't get an itinerary before now is beyond me.'

'Same way he convinced the police not to conduct a proper enquiry into Marine's death,' I said. 'By persuading them that he'll properly look into it at the school - and then not.'

Simon coughed, nodding. 'You find in these cases, Ben,' he said, 'that all of the administrative methods used in professional circles-confidentiality, whatever else is in vogue, are just tools. Tools that governing bodies can deploy, under the guise of fairness. Some of the most corrupt organisations I have worked with have the most finely developed guidelines that they work to. These guidelines give them more rope to hang their victims.' Simon stood up. 'I'll make some calls to push for a public hearing now,' he said, padding his pockets for his mobile. 'I'll have to put the fear of God into them, drop in a few mentions about the petition. I have no idea if that'll work, but it's worth a shot.'

'Definitely,' I said, as he passed by me to go into the kitchen. 'Katy and Lorraine said they weren't prepared to do more than work behind the scenes,' I said. 'But if the hearing is made public I bet they won't mind being in the crowd.'

'You could even call on them, if needs be?' Simon said.

'I don't want to force them to risk their jobs.'

'Well, fortunately for you, Juliette's petition has revealed the weight of public opinion about the school's behaviour. So Katy and Lorraine would no longer be risking their jobs, as Kraver can't argue that they're just making trouble. The public has already made enough noise to confirm that there is a valid issue here.'

'I can convince them,' Juliette said, bringing a silver carafe of coffee in. With her hair tied up, a new flush of colour was visible in her face. 'In fact,' she said, 'I will phone and tell them that we might be close to victory, but we need their help.'

'I hope you win them over. They both have pretty powerful roles to play in all this,' Art said. 'And from what I can tell about this Kraver character, if you don't have them present I guess he'll argue that their confidentiality must be protected, and that we can't mention them during the hearing.'

'Even if they supply written consent?'

He laughed. 'Oh yes. He'd love to create a barrier to them getting mentioned, in any way he can. This–' he gestured at Bracewell in the doorway. 'Lorraine Hogan is it?'

'Hannerty,' I said.

'I'm new to all this legal stuff,' Art breezed. 'Anyway, this Hannerty could, in effect, play the role of a character witness. Showing the panel what a bully Kraver is. But Katy Fergus is key. We must get her over and drill her,' he said, raising his voice to Juliette, who, ensconced on the phone, acknowledged his shout with a thumbs-up. 'You see, the key part of this enquiry will be stopping it becoming a character assassination of you, Ben. It's most important that we turn the spotlight on the conduct of Kraver, and the school. Katy must put across the evidence she has about Walker and this CRB malarkey. It'll be key to getting the panel to move the game onto the playing field that we want to play on. Problem is, it is very difficult to get an agenda changed. If you're seen as trying to change the items on the agenda, Ben, they can argue that you did not engage with the process, which would be very dangerous. You can only do it if the public anger visible at the hearing becomes too great for them to ignore. But if we do move the focus onto Kraver, you'll need to speak very passionately about what he's done to you.'

There is so much to remember, I thought, easing into Juliette's seat. I had a sudden urge to grip the chair and not move. What would happen, I wondered, if I just stayed in the chair? The determination to stay immobile grew stronger. I had the same feeling as when I'd stood on that bridge. In a way, the fight felt even more futile now than it did then. Who were we kidding, trying to put together an alliance more complex than our enemy? No, I thought. I won't halt this momentum with my own cynicism. I need to be a leader now. Or at the very least resemble one. I thought of my revelation in the bathroom, during that dark night. How I made the decision that a family was made of building blocks. I looked Art straight in the eye.

'I want to give him both barrels,' I said. 'It wasn't so long ago that I was fighting this alone. Now I have all of you on board the last thing I'm going to do is let you down.'

Art jumped up clapped a hand on my shoulder. 'Atta boy,' he croaked. 'That's exactly the spirit we need. But there's just one more thing you need to remember. In these hearings you can always sense, early on, if the outcome is yet to be decided, or if has already been made. Admittedly, my experience of this type of hearing is limited. But I've sometimes been at awards ceremonies with clients of mine, and we're genuinely thinking they're going to win. But a wink here, a hand clasp there, and you get a clear sense that the whole affair has already been sewn up.'

'What do we do if that happens?' I asked.

'We tear open the stitches,' he said, raising his glass.

Bracewell came in with a smile on his face.

'What is it?' I asked.

'I've just had word from my assistant,' he said. 'The coroner has, in response to the petition, recommended that the CPS reopen the enquiry into Marine's death and consider the possibility of criminal charges.'

'You're kidding,' I said. 'That is great news.'

'That'll put Kraver on the run tomorrow,' Art said. He mimed a man turning a huge lamp around, onto me. 'The spotlight has begun its slow revolution round, onto him,' he said.

'There's more,' Bracewell said, puffing his chest out. I imagined him as a cricketer, defending a vital wicket. Bat poised, glint in his eye. 'The coroner has also criticized the police for following the advice of Kraver and not investigating *everyone* involved in the field trip.'

'I don't believe it,' I said. I turned to Juliette, who was entering the room. 'Isn't that brilliant?'

'Katy and Lorraine will be there,' she said.

'That can't have been easy,' I said, shooting Juliette a look of admiration. The fragile student I had first met would never have made such a call, I thought.

'It's nothing compared with what you have to do, for us,' she said.

I smiled back at her. 'And Marine,' I said.

+ + + + +

It was 10 p.m. by the time everyone left. Juliette's fixed expression betrayed that she was rallying her mental forces as much as she could. I could see fear in her eyes, fear that perhaps tomorrow my career would be rubber-stamped as 'over'. As I removed my slippers on the end of the bed, she fussed in the kitchen, tidying and re-tidying. I barely heard our letter box bang, and I was too tired to wonder who was posting something to us at this time.

I rolled under the sheets and called out to Juliette. It was only after five minutes without a response that I wondered what could have been posted. Calling her name I got out of the bed, and padded into the kitchen.

Juliette was looking up at the ceiling. In one hand she was holding an A4 envelope. In her other hand she was grasping what appeared to be a sheaf of photographs.

'What is it?' I said, rubbing my eye. 'Why aren't you coming to bed?'

'Because of this,' she said, in a low voice.

She handed me the black and white pictures.

The first was of me following Violet into her house. A broad smile on my face, my hand on her back. The picture had, in the bottom right hand corner of it, the date and time.

'Juliette, I–'

'Keep looking,' she said.

I flicked through the other photographs. They were dated two days previous and showed Violet and me laughing over a cup of tea in a café. In one, her hand appeared clasped over mine. She was looking deep into my eyes.

The final photo showed the door closing behind me as I went into Violet's apartment block. A cold chill shivered down my back when I saw that, in the photo Violet, seemed to be glancing directly at the camera. As if she not only knew the photographer was there. But as if she had been expecting them.

I felt blood drain from my face. The ground beneath my feet grew weak.

'Juliette, there is an explanation.'

'I can't even look at you right now.' She looked at the ceiling again. 'I honestly can't even look at you right now.'

'You know that they are doing this to undermine our fight for Marine tomorrow? Don't you?'

I could see her attempting to measure each word, one at a time. 'And you think carrying on with this girl is what Marine would have wanted?' She shook her heard fiercely. 'Who is she, Ben?'

'A friend of Phillip's.'

Her eyes flashed to Christian's room as she narrowed her eyes onto me.

'Some *slut* that you and him are passing between you?'

'This is what they want us to do, Juliette,' I said, deciding not to take her hand as I wanted to. Kraver has me right where he wants me, I thought. Again. 'You have to trust me,' I said. 'She *is* a friend. I did let her in too much, after you threw me out of the house. But I have got a grip on it now.'

'You are joking? There is no way you are trying to justify–'

I put my arm on her shoulder, but she shuddered away from it. 'Come on,' I said. 'Don't let them win.'

She shook her head, moisture building in the corner of her eye. The eyeliner was crumbling. 'How can you say that–' she said, her voice breaking.

'Say what?'

'That I'll *let them win*. Let me tell you something, Ben. I am going to pretend, for one night, that I believe you. It is going to take all my strength, but I need to believe it right now. I need to believe it because I need us to get through tomorrow. Because whatever happens we are *not* going to let them win.'

I hung my head. 'You're right,' she said.

She moved closer. I caught the scent of spearmint on her breath. 'You are going to beat them tomorrow, Ben. Do you understand me?'

I nodded.

That night, I barely slept at all. I thought for hours about what Violet had said. They had been digging for dirt on me, and I had stupidly given them something to find. But what was so awful, as I lay there on the couch, was that I wasn't even able to marshal a sense of determination. I needed to go to sleep, to be ready for the fight of my life the next day. But all I could think about was that final photo. Had they somehow recruited, Violet to break up my family?

Why had she been looking at the camera?

TWENTY-THREE

THE FOLLOWING DAY, I stood in my dressing gown in the kitchen, barely able to move. Bracewell was sat, in the seating area of the lounge, where Marine had once scrambled. Then, it had been called 'The Den'. Recently, we had renamed it 'The War Room'.

He had arrived at 9 a.m. to take me through the charges that I would have to defend myself against. Juliette hadn't yet emerged from the bedroom. I could only guess at the trials she had mentally put herself through in the night, thanks to me.

Just as Bracewell predicted, the charges had arrived in the post only that morning. He had intercepted the postman, scouring the streets for a distant flash of red.

'Can we not call them out on that?' I said.

'They'll find some email address of yours they sent it to, knowing you wouldn't check it. Perhaps your teaching one?'

'Which they've banned me from using.'

'There we have it,' he said.

I noticed slender, dark rings under his eyes, and I cursed myself for not carefully checking how much money we had already spent on him. Given the strain of preparing, and the balancing act I had to keep up with Phillip, Violet and Juliette, I hadn't attended to such practicalities. Even if I won, would I still be paying him off when I was an old man?

We tried to settle in, him opposite me in a sharp suit whilst I reclined, exhausted, on the sofa. In the distance I could hear a car alarm, which wouldn't turn off.

'You look wrecked,' he said.

'Thanks,' I snapped.

'Rough night?'

I nodded.

'I've had word that Katy and Lorraine will be coming to the hearing,' he said, unzipping his glossy leather briefcase. 'Also, I got an email late yesterday, with the news that the teachers' association have reluctantly agreed for the hearing to be made public.'

I heard Juliette wordlessly slamming items down. 'Is she alright?' he said.

'Let's just focus on getting ready, Simon,' I answered.

I forced myself to my feet whilst Bracewell chugged through the charges. He stopped, every now and again, distracted by Juliette's slamming, audible from various rooms. 'What's *wrong* with her?' he said.

'This is really getting to all of us now,' I said, realizing that if she told Phillip about Violet I might see myself losing my partner, best friend and job all in one day. 'Whatever happens, it has to end today.'

Perhaps detecting something, Bracewell smiled sympathetically. 'It will. You're doing well,' he said. 'There aren't simply right moves and wrong moves, there's more to it than that. Every move takes you further away from what this should all be about– which is

Marine. This is a game that moves as you play, and one that hurts as you play, too.'

'I agree,' I said.

'You don't think she'll do anything to undermine you, do you?' he asked, looking over my shoulder.

'Don't talk about her like that, Simon,' I said. 'She's made of tougher stuff than you or I.' He widened his eyes, and I rubbed my forehead. 'I'm sorry I'm snappy,' I said.

He dismissed the apology with a shake of his head, turned to the charge sheet, and tapped it. 'So. This is just full of the kind of low shots and exaggerations we prepped for, Ben,' he said. 'Item one, "use of social media to libel character of Paul Kraver". It says you were an argumentative member of staff, which I can see no evidence of this morning, and that you sometimes indulged in devious behaviour.'

'That'll be the dressing in drag,' Juliette said, appearing in the doorway.

Her face was scrubbed of makeup, and she looked more exposed, more vulnerable, than I had seen her allow herself to be with strangers before.

Bracewell continued to read. 'It says you took sick leave that wasn't agreed, made errors in administration, and didn't take sufficient breaks.' He began reading in an officious tone. "The panel will decide, given the evidence, if they should advise the Department of Education that the Interim Prohibition Order against you be made permanent", and you'll hear two days after the hearing what they decide. It's all just what we expected.'

'This is your only chance, Ben,' Juliette said, taking a sip of coffee. Her eyes narrowed. 'Don't forget that.'

TWENTY-FOUR

IT WAS A COOL, brightening morning. As we approached the car park I could see in the distance a group of harried-looking parents, a hunched tapestry of coats, shielding themselves from the wind. When they saw me they gave out a low cheer. This prompted a flurry of car doors to open, and within a few moments a mob of photographers and reporters were surrounding me, microphones and video camera pointing in my direction. 'Mr Pendleton, can you spare us a comment?' one shouted. The others started firing questions at me.

'What do you have to say to Paul Kraver?' a bearded man asked, jostling in front of a Dictaphone. 'He's had plenty to say to us about you.'

'My client has no comment to make at this time,' Bracewell said, patting the air. 'Please, give my client the room to get inside.'

Inside the building Lorraine, Katy and Phillip responded to my greeting with the kind of cautiousness that suggested hidden concern. We were directed, by a pallid receptionist I didn't know, into a first-floor room, where more new staff were laying out rows of chairs that faced a raised platform. The parents filed into chairs, their sudden movements denoting a willingness to kick off. I wondered why they had refrained from talking to me outside.

I was directed, by the receptionist, to sit at the end of the front row of chairs, with Juliette, Lorraine, Katy and Bracewell sitting with muted expressions beside me. On the raised dais five chairs had been placed in front of a table, which held a half-full jug of water and some school tumblers, heavily scratched from the dishwasher. The words 'kangaroo court' flashed into my mind – I half fancied for a moment that I was about to watch a school production of Kafka's 'The Trial'.

It was then that Phillip entered, smiling apologetically, as he took a seat next to Juliette. 'Just speak clearly and confidently,' Juliette whispered, to me. 'You can't afford to let us down any more.'

Phillip overheard her warning. 'Everything alright here?' he asked, looking between us.

'I got some rather unpleasant news last night,' Juliette said, sourly. ·

'What was it?' Phillip said.

Juliette looked at me. 'Ben?'

From behind me, a male parent with a strong hand clapped me on the back. 'You give 'em hell, lad,' he said.

'What's going on, Ben?' Phillip asked, again.

The door opened. Three men and a woman entered in front of Kraver, and moved towards to their seats on the stage. Kraver, wearing a double-breasted suit that looked new, assumed the role of usher. Once the panel had filed into their seats, he perched himself on the end of them. He looked steadily at me, addressing me in a tone that suggested I possessed variable mental faculties.

'Good morning, good morning, good morning,' he said, pulling his jacket around him. This man here,' he said, motioning to the man on my far left, 'is Ian Preston, who has kindly agreed to appear on the panel because he is something of a dab hand in these disciplinary matters. He will be offering us some oversight, and he's here to just make sure there is no damage done to the reputation of the education body.'

Preston was bald, with white-rimmed glasses. He flashed a tight smile at me as he weaved his fingers together on the desk.

'No guesses as to who Kraver's plant is then,' Simon whispered.

Kraver heard the whisper and turned to Bracewell. 'Right then, Mr. Bracewell,' he said, his voice sharp. 'I know that as Mr. Pendleton's legal representative you are looking forward to earning your stripes today, and we will give you the chance to speak. But we will only hear you when you speak as instructed. We must stick to certain practical and rational considerations, and I've found in my experience that when we do it all becomes very straightforward.'

'I understand,' Bracewell said, politely.

'One important consideration is that this session will last for two hours, and it must end sharply at 1 p.m., mind, as this room has been booked by someone else.'

The parents in the seats gave off a low buzz of protest. I realized that they had filled the room, and the new arrivals were having to squeeze in at the back.

'I must raise an objection to that,' Bracewell said. 'This hearing is to decide the fate of one man's career. You can't honestly expect us to be troubled by a room booking?'

'Mr. Bracewell,' Kraver continued, closing his eyes, 'I see you're already getting out of your box and we haven't yet started. I'm assuming you don't want to be kicked out? No?'

To my amazement, Bracewell shook his head.

'Good, good, that's all dandy, and I will now hand you over to the chair of this meeting, Chris Manning.'

'Thank you, Mr Kraver,' said the portly man sitting next to Preston. Manning's hand was clasped to his chin, with the forefinger pointed at the ceiling. The intensity of his gaze suggested a powerful intellect. But the slight hangdog look also suggested some sort of shame about its use.

'Joining me on the panel,' Manning said, 'is Angela Glass.' He gestured to a woman next to him who, despite her glossy, dark hair, possessed a slightly masculine muscularity. The final chair, next to Kraver, was filled by a man who suddenly introduced himself as 'Rupert Morris, legal advisor'. The moment he spoke he raised his chin. His nasal wine seemed to pre-empt a disagreement that had not yet happened.

He and Bracewell eyed each other carefully, two cats ready to fight over an already promised ball of wool. Morris seemingly noticed something behind me. 'I am afraid I must ask members of the public not to film,' he said.

'Why not?' said the man behind me. 'This is a public interest case. Isn't that why it is open to the public?'

'Under law,' Morris said, in an ingratiating tone, 'an employee cannot say anything that damages his employer's reputation. Recording this hearing would facilitate that.'

'I'll tweet instead then,' said a woman at his side, raising a couple of cheers.

'Now,' Manning said. 'We will begin by Mr Kraver taking us through the items which have raised concern about Mr. Pendleton's Fitness to Practice.'

Those words, now issued without any contextual balm, stung more than I expected.

'We will start,' he said, 'with points that have been raised since the informal hearing.'

+ + + + +

'The first, and most immediate concern, is that in recent days, you have used a television interview to slander the school. In so doing you have not only destroyed the hard work of all members of staff involved in the documentary about the school, but you have brought the good name of the school into disrepute. You are therefore in violation of Section 4d of your teaching contract. How do you answer the charge?'

'I did not wish to bring the school into disrepute,' I began. 'My main motivation for doing the TV interview was to bring to the attention of the public the fact that my daughter was killed during an outing at an affiliated school.'

Kraver straightened his back. 'And in the aftermath of her death,' I continued, 'various people, such as Katy Fergus and Lorraine Hannerty, brought to my attention that one of the Teaching Assistants present that day, David Walker, had a history of convictions against children, which the school had not properly investigated.'

'I must intervene,' said Morris, leaning over to Manning. 'This response, in a public setting is clearly intended to bring the school into further disrepute, thus enforcing the chair's claim.'

His nonchalance made my heartbeat quicken. 'The CPS have decided,' I continued, 'as a result of the coroner reopening the case into my daughter's death, to instruct the police to now *fully* investigate what happened on the day she fell.'

'The school spent every penny it could practically afford looking into that,' Kraver said. 'Unless you want the children to be taught using slate and chalk, there is nothing more we could do. Is that what the parents would want?'

The parents bridled.

'Noted,' said Manning.

'With me today,' I continued, 'is another teacher at the school, Katy Fergus. She was present on the day of the accident and she has found evidence that Mr Walker, under a previous name, was found guilty of offences against children–'

'Mr. Pendleton…' Manning said, interrupting.

'Out of the question,' said Kraver.

'Whilst under a previous name,' I continued. 'She is willing to present evidence now, that Mr. Kraver was *informed* about this.'

'Out of the question, pure fiction,' Kraver said.

'–but decided not to investigate it,' I finished.

The panel consulted.

'Given that this case is still being investigated by the CPS,' Manning eventually said, 'the panel propose that this point of contention is irrelevant until their investigation is completed. This is a hearing to discuss and decide upon Mr Pendleton's Fitness to Practice, not a court of law. Therefore the evidence of Miss Fergus is not relevant today.'

'It certainly is,' Bracewell said, his voice loud.

Morris whispered something to Manning.

'That is the decision of the panel, Mr Bracewell,' Manning said. 'As Mr. Morris has quite rightly just pointed out to me, the evidence from other staff members is confidential, and therefore not in the interests of the greater good.'

'But I waive my right to confidentiality!' Katy shouted, from a row behind me.

'Even if you do, Miss Fergus,' Manning said, 'that does not mean your opinion can be taken on board today.'

'It is completely relevant!' she said, to rising cheers from the audience. 'What I have to say undercuts the premise of the whole case against Ben!'

The panel consulted again. 'As the panel consult,' Kraver said, wriggling in his chair, 'I would just like to say something, if that's okay. There's been a lot of changes at this school since I took over and I know, I know, some people don't like change. They like everything to stay the same it was. It's easy to resist the brush of a clean broom, but I ask the parents not to let their fear of change stop them having faith in me.' He pressed his hands against his heart. 'Trust me,' he said, 'don't push against me.'

The parents chattered amongst themselves.

'To press on with why we are here,' Manning said, clearing his throat, 'the second point on the agenda is that, whilst suspended, Mr Pendleton used his on-going pay from the school to attack it. He thereby exploited the resources of the school. Can you confirm for us, Mr Pendleton, whether you were paid for your television appearance?'

I consulted with Bracewell. 'My client has no knowledge of any payment he will receive,' he said.

Kraver, with a broad smile, handed Manning a piece of paper.

Manning cast an eye over it, handed it to his neighbour, and looked up. 'I ask the panel to consider the evidence offered here by Mr Kraver. It details the payment that guests on the Craig Peterson show are paid for their appearance. It is a lot of money.'

A boo rang out behind me. 'He was raising awareness of the school's cover-up!' shouted the man behind me.

'And making a pretty penny,' a woman hissed.

'There will be time for questions at the end,' Manning said. 'For the record, I ask for it to be noted that evidence has just been supplied which proves how much Mr. Pendleton was paid for his television appearance. Mr Kraver feels this offers us some relevant insight into Mr Pendleton's character.'

'That's preposterous,' I said. 'To accuse me of using my daughter to make money. I haven't received a penny.'

'You may find it outrageous, but we have to act on evidence,' Manning said. 'I take it there is no response to that charge then? So, the next point is that as a teacher you were known for some aggressive behaviour, in particular towards your line manager.'

'Does the evidence here relate purely to evidence from my line manager, Mr. Kraver?' I asked.

Manning consulted with Kraver. 'Today, it does,' he said.

I tried to push through my confusion. 'Then I have to answer that question by asking Lorraine Hannerty to speak. Hannerty was, in the wake of my daughter's death, quickly relocated to another campus after it became clear that she was the source of this knowledge about Mr Walker–'

'As I have made clear,' Manning said. 'The events of that day are not relevant to this hearing, and as I have already pointed out, neither are matters which we have to consider confidential.' Kraver whispered into his ear. 'I am also conscious that we have less than two hours and more charges against Mr Pendleton which we must hear. We must follow the established process.'

'This is getting out of hand,' I said, to Bracewell.

'You've got to say something,' Juliette hissed at him.

Bracewell clutched his papers and stood up. 'This objection must be heard,' he said, his voice faltering. 'Given that the teachers' association have deemed this hearing in the public interest, the chair must, in all fairness concede, that in order to determine my client's fitness we understand fully the provocations he has been subjected to.' The parents hummed in approval. Buoyed, Bracewell spoke more clearly. 'They have clearly led to any behaviour he is now having to answer for,' he finished.

The parents roared their approval. They stamped their feet, and clapped their hands. The shock on Manning's face, at their reaction, seemed to only amplify their shouts. As they increased in volume it occurred to me that Manning had no choice but to accept this point. He had to now hear my criticisms of Kraver, or the meeting would descend into farce.

'The power of the people,' Phillip said, leaning over to me. 'You can't crush it, Che.'

'I can see passions are running high,' said Manning. 'And I don't want this to turn into a Saturday night chat show. So I now ask for a short intermission whilst the panel convene to discuss this matter.'

+ + + + +

Bracewell turned sharply to me, as everyone turned to their neighbour to review. 'It is pretty evident to me that the plant here is Manning, not Preston,' he said. 'How Kraver has arranged that, I have no idea, but I think what they are doing by consulting here, is running down the clock. This two-hour time limit is completely arbitrary, considering the high amount of public interest in this matter. They just want to create time limits to ensure that little mud can be thrown at them. And all that talk about confidentiality was desperate stuff. We might be starting to get some movement here, Ben.'

'I'm not so sure,' I said.

'You should be,' Bracewell said. 'But what you will find is that now they have opened themselves to criticism, they will have to change their tactics. I think you'll find the charges against you from now on to be long and rambling, so they can run down the clock. That will give the public less time to have their say.'

I was surprised by his cynicism, but the buzzing in my chest gave me no choice but to just agree with him. When the panel reconvened, Manning's charges about me – from my errors in administration to my not taking breaks – were needlessly verbose. My objections were as passionate as I could make them but Kraver seemed to enjoy my anger. Whenever it seemed as though I was about to land a punch on him, he'd just lean into Manning and whisper to him. The response of Manning would then be that 'the school is being victimized.'

I realized then how carefully Kraver had arranged the geography of this next part of the hearing. He had positioned himself next to Manning, so he could play courtier to the king. Each accusation was delivered by Manning, with Kraver's constant vitriol driving him on, like a spur in his side. I knew I could not address Kraver personally, but only through Manning. Any point I wanted to make had to be funnelled through the small channels of fake formality. I decided to ram my argument into those channels so hard that I would break them.

'I have only one answer to these accusations,' I said, once the charges had been laid out. 'If this hearing has so many good reasons to attack me, then why have over a million people signed a petition? A petition arguing that the school should *stop* attacking me and *start* looking instead into how my daughter was killed?'

Roars of agreement came from behind me. They were almost feral in their intensity. Kraver opened his mouth to speak, but decided to bide his time.

'If the charges against me,' I continued, shouting above the noise, 'for making errors in my administration, for taking too few breaks, are so powerful, then why are the people behind me screaming their encouragement as I call this hearing to account?'

Phillip, Juliette, Katy, and then Lorraine stood up and applauded. Manning looked over at Kraver, who leant forward.

'It is wrong to play on people's fears ...' he began.

I decided it was my turn to not let him speak.

'Why, if I am such a bad apple, do so many people feel there is a serious miscarriage of justice going on here, with the school *covering up* their incompetence by allowing a *criminal* to supervise my daughter? Then *whitewashing* their investigation, and attacking *me*, instead of having the guts to address the matter?'

Kraver had a sudden spasm of movement. It was the first time his mask of calm had slipped. I momentarily wondered if I had at last landed a blow. Battling to make himself heard against the cheers, and with the panel turning to him in surprise, Kraver answered me directly. 'Perhaps because you saw an opportunity to exploit the hard work of others to make yourself money!' he hissed.

Manning shot him a look.

'*The Crown Prosecution Service*,' I shouted, raising my voice above the loudening roars, 'have decided that *you* convinced the police not to fully investigate my daughter's death, and so they have reopened their investigation. And yet still you–' I said, pointing at Kraver, 'argue that I am the guilty party. You are *embarrassing* yourself, and this fine school!'

Kraver's jaw dropped. He looked unable to speak. I remembered then, in a flash of inspiration, Violet's advice.

'Look, he can't even answer!' I shouted, looking around me.

The people behind me got to their feet and cheered. 'You should step down!' a man shouted. 'You're a disgrace!'

'You employed a paedophile!' one woman screamed.

'Please,' Manning said, patting his hands against the air. 'I ask for calm!'

'You've tried to railroad me into accepting a false narrative, and tried to hoodwink these good people. And you wonder why they are in uproar!' I shouted.

The blood was surging in my veins. It was pulsing hard in my temple. At that moment, I knew I had changed. I was no longer the shy man who clammed up in public. I was no longer a man who steadied himself in bathrooms. I had fury in my heart, fire in my mouth, and the love of my daughter keeping me strong. Juliette looked up at me. Her lips were trembling.

'Mr Pendleton, please,' Manning said. 'It is only fair you allow Mr Kraver the opportunity to answer.'

'Let me just say, to the panel, and to all the fine people who have taken their time to come here today,' Kraver said, 'that I agree with you. *No one* welcomes more than me this police investigation into what happened on that school outing. If the CPS, and the board of governors, feel we have the resources to investigate that day more fully then let me tell you, no one is happier about that than I.'

'You liar,' Juliette whispered. She repeated herself, the insult louder this time. Amongst the din her voice rang out, clear.

I realized then that she had changed too. She spoke with such confidence that even Kraver, with all his resources, could not look her in the eye. He could not respond to a mother's pain with only his self-interest.

'Can we improve the processes we have here?' Kraver continued, his voice thin with strain. 'Yes. Must we improve them? Damn right we must.'

'He is trying to run down the clock,' Bracewell said. 'It's so obvious.'

'You should stand down! Resign now, man, you're an embarrassment!' one mother shouted.

'Will you stand down?' the man behind me roared.

The clamour was so great, that he had to answer. I sat back, enjoying the moment. The worm was being pinned.

'I don't answer to a mob,' Kraver said, his voice hoarse. 'I answer only to the board of governors. And while they have full confidence in me, I will carry on doing a job which, by the way, I have been praised for. And one of my first priorities will be to examine the processes which all need to improve.'

'You were the one who corrupted these processes. How can you improve them?' the man shouted.

'People, please,' Manning said.

'Why won't the man answer the question!' the man shouted. 'If anyone should be being scrutinized it's you!'

'I have answered the question about Mr Walker before, and this is not the time for me to do that again,' Kraver said. 'It's been dealt with, and I won't rake up old graves.'

'That is very interesting,' Bracewell said, sweeping his papers to one side. 'Do you have any evidence of when that matter was dealt with, Mr Kraver? On what date? After all, it could form part of the police investigation. An investigation which is inching ever closer to you.'

The cheers were now almost deafening.

'People, please!' Manning shouted. 'This hearing is no longer serving the function it was intended to. Our time is up.'

The voices quietened.

'I will now ask the panel to adjourn,' he said.

The volume fell. I noticed a thin sheen of sweat on his brow. 'We will come to a decision regarding Mr Pendleton and his Fitness to Practice,' he said.

His voice was thin with strain.

TWENTY-FIVE

THE OUTCOME OF the hearing came through by post two days later.

In those intervening days I barely ate or slept. I wasn't tired though – it was almost as if I was in a state of suspended animation. During those long, waking hours I thought hard about what to do if I was declared unfit to teach. On the one hand I could continue to fight the attacks on me. But on the other hand, if it was decided that I shouldn't teach, perhaps I should accept that. Perhaps I then needed to see that all along I had been wrong, and that what I had deemed attacks on me were in fact a fair evaluation. It terrified me to think that all I had taken as true might have been false – and that a single typed letter in the post might be about to decide that.

When the letter arrived on the doormat, I somehow knew it contained the verdict. As I stood with it, Juliette huddled behind me. I felt her warmth infusing my back. With shaking hands, I tore the letter open so quickly that I ripped off the top corner of the page.

'The panel, after much debate, found Mr Pendleton fit to return to work,' I read.

Juliette let out a sob. As she kissed my cheek, I felt a tear squash against my nose. Whether it was from her or me, I don't really know. I felt shored up, and that the core of my life had become firm again. I could pay Bracewell - eventually. We could pay our mortgage. I could keep this precious, three-legged animal that I called my family out of the cold.

'You did it,' she said, running her hands through her hair. 'You beat them, Ben. Oh my God, I'm shaking. I can't believe it. We have our life back. It's over.'

It was only when the shaking in my hands had subsided that I sat down and inspected the letter.

'No mention, of Kraver being investigated,' I said.

'Have you seen how many people tweeted about it on the day? All the coverage that was online?' Juliette began to pace around the room as she spoke, her excitement building. I couldn't remember having seen her like this before, her hands circling animatedly as she moved. 'The board of directors will have to look into his behaviour now, won't they?' she urged.

I decided to dismiss my cynicism. I stepped over, and held her by the shoulders. My relentless, shaking Juliette, who had battled through this with me. 'We did it,' I said. 'We actually did it.'

She nodded, her mouth trembling. 'You have to return to the school with your head held high,' she said. 'It'll be very hard for Kraver to cling to his job now.'

But Kraver did cling to his job. Even though the local papers were full of the news story in the days that followed, Kraver was quoted sounding as defiant as ever. 'It's always been my wish for there to be a thorough investigation into the death of Marine Pendleton', I read, at a windswept newspaper stand. I had to trace over the words, scarcely believing they belonged on the page. How could one person stand against a tide of justice for so long, and then pretend to be a part of it? In the picture he seemed to have put on weight. 'As the headmaster of this fine school,' he'd said, 'I look forward to continuing to assist in these investigations in every single way that I can. This school won over the hearts of a nation, and it won't be long before I remind us once more how it did that.'

The newspaper journalist had asked how he could be expected to clear up a mess that he had presided over. 'I have the full confidence of the board of directors,' he said, 'and it is my responsibility to now guide the school out of troubled waters and see that we start to make headlines only for the very best reasons. And I have not one shred of doubt that I am the man to steer that boat.'

+ + + + +

Bracewell, invigorated perhaps by his impending paycheque, arrived early at our house a week later.

Christian had been recently getting into trouble at school, and as part of our strategy to handle the situation I'd been spending more and more time with him in the mornings. Strangely enough, I felt echoes of Marine in Christian around that time. Christian had just started telling me about his imaginary friend, 'Boogaloo', as he finished his cereal. This morning Boogaloo was sad, he said. His sadness seemed to be infecting Christian with a sense of lethargy, as he didn't want to go to school. It was an argument Marine used to make.

I was about to ask him more when I saw Bracewell's silver Lexus park smoothly outside. Bracewell flashed glances in either direction before tucking his raincoat into itself, and crossing the road to our door.

'Juliette?' I called, prompting her to rush out from the bedroom.

She was still in her ivory nightgown. 'Bracewell has just arrived,' I said.

Juliette didn't seem to mind the sudden intrusion now - perhaps she had grown used to our home having an open door.

Bracewell unleashed a passionate flow of words soon as I opened the door.

'The evidence found by Katy Fergus led to the police to finally *fully* evaluate all the evidence they collected on the day Marine fell,' he began.

His eyes were shining as he looked between us for our reaction. 'You're fortunate,' he gushed, stepping inside, 'because in the US improperly obtained evidence could be deemed inadmissible. But after some deliberation it was decided that Katy Fergus' evidence about Walker should be looked at. The police began to properly investigate his past.'

'Hold on a moment,' I said, leading Christian into the next room.

I returned moments later. Bracewell was sat down. His side parting had, for the first time, fallen over his eyes but he didn't try to sweep it back. I imagined him at the cricket crease, steeling himself for the swings that would inch him to victory.

He looked up at Juliette and me, impassively standing there. 'On the day of her death the Senior Investigating Officer prudently decided to collect clothing samples from all involved, including Walker,' he said. 'He also got the Crime Scene Investigators to collect evidence from the crime scene. Why they didn't properly evaluate it at the time is beyond me. My guess is that Kraver somehow persuaded them not to. But Katy's evidence unblocked that particular problem. Having dug into Walker's past, they found that the attack he was convicted of, in his previous life, had been on a girl. What's more it had been on a windy, deserted moor. The psychologist's conclusion was that Walker was trying to recreate that attack with Marine regardless of the likelihood that he would succeed.'

Juliette clasped her hand to her mouth.

'I know this is hard, but I must get this out,' Bracewell pressed, folding his fingers. 'The police decided to look at Walker's digital fingerprint. They seized his phone, his computer, and looked for evidence that he had some sort of pathological, psychological makeup. They found some trophy photographs that he had taken of the young girl he attacked, and they decided that she bore some similarity to Marine. The police psychologist believes that his attack on Marine was not pre-meditated, but a spontaneous act, which led to him trying to separate her from the other girls.'

I shook my head.

'Now the police investigations had some direction,' he said, 'they decided to evaluate the clothing they had obtained from Walker on the day. Although some time had passed, they managed to find matching DNA, from Walker, on the clothing that Marine had on when she died.'

'I hope it was conclusive,' I said.

'Well, Walker's lawyer argued that it wasn't,' he said. 'His argument was, "My client's DNA was found on Marine because Walker had to physically make contact on her to pull her back from the cliff edge." But the fabrics analyst found that the majority of the DNA from Walker, on Marine, was left around her waist. Suggesting that he had in fact been trying to remove her clothing.'

'Marine must have been terrified,' Juliette said, her voice hollow.

Bracewell nodded. 'There's more. Further evidence of Walker's guilt was that the police proved he had dropped his gloves on the moor, in the area between the path and the cliff edge. Questions were asked about why Walker would have felt a need to remove his gloves at all. It was concluded that it was all part of his attempted attack on Marine. Walker – unsurprisingly – refuted this. He reasserted that he had seen her fall from the cliff edge from some distance.'

He zipped open his briefcase and leafed rapidly through a file. 'But "the Area Forensic Manager",' he said, quoting, '"conducted a Blood Spatter Analysis which concluded that Marine ran off the cliff, rather than fell". This all added to the narrative she had built up, which described how Walker kept her back from other children on the pretext of showing her flowers, before trying to attack her. The forensic specialist offered the professional opinion that Marine ran away from Walker, and that because he continued to pursue her she ended up *running* from the cliff edge.'

Juliette bowed her head.

'That must have been enough to convict?' I ventured.

'There was more. And the "more" proves that it was worth your while, Ben, to fight so hard for justice.'

He seemed to direct the statement solely at me. As Juliette looked up, her expression bridling, I couldn't help wondering what he had decided about our relationship.

'Go on,' I said.

'Walker left a footprint at the scene of the fall. Police were able to match it, using something called the "UK National Footwear Database", to four unsolved attacks on young children in the region. They dated back almost five years. As a result of all this, a very dangerous, predatory man has finally been arrested.'

'Did he hurt Marine?' Juliette asked.

'No, there is no evidence whatsoever that he did hurt Marine – in that way.'

'Do they still think she died quickly?' she asked.

'Instantly,' he said, handing her the post-mortem report.

'Her last moments were lived in absolute terror,' Juliette said, taking it.

'Brief terror,' Bracewell said, with a sympathetic smile. 'If it's any consolation, the evidence that he didn't harm her is conclusive.'

'He killed her,' Juliette said, quietly.

Bracewell nodded softly. 'The police, finally, agree with your verdict. The coroner has now changed the verdict on Marine's death to "unlawful killing". Walker is going to prison.'

'What about Kraver?' I asked.

Bracewell inhaled, and leant back.

'I find him if not equally responsible, then certainly culpable,' I said.

'Well, you now have proven grounds to sue both the school and Kraver if you so wish. Kraver has always known you were right, or he'd have sued you after the TV show. The school has been found guilty of errors of process, but no one has been arrested for that.'

'Can we not get him for perverting the course of justice? He clearly convinced the police not to look at any of his staff. They didn't even examine the evidence they'd collected.'

'Unfortunately, it seems the police do not have sufficient evidence that Kraver perverted the course of justice. If the school want to suspend him, they can. But somehow he… is clinging on. Perhaps, and I am going out on a limb here - Kraver has some leverage that we don't know about.'

'Course he does.'

Bracewell nodded. 'Even though this case has been widely reported in the press, and even though parents are boycotting the school, Kraver seems to have been able to convince the board of governors that he really is the man to fix this mess.'

'That just doesn't make sense.'

'As Kraver said in your hearing, he is answerable only to the board of governors. Everyone in the world can think him immoral and guilty, from the staff to the parents, to the pupils, to the janitors. But we live in a bureaucratic world, where we are all tamed by these invisible systems. Unless three of those governors change their minds he still has the job.'

'I find it impossible to get my head around that.'

'Ben,' he said, scratching his temple. 'I've represented whistle-blowers in the NHS. In cases where it was proven that chief executives were hiring detectives to smear whistle-blowers and discredit them. Using millions of pounds worth of taxpayers' money to do that. These executives have clung to their jobs even after that has hit the papers. We live in a culture of deferred accountability. These people don't just get sacked, they can get promoted, knighted, handed large pensions. Pensions funded by hardworking people. You can't change the culture. Cover-ups of this kind happen in banking and healthcare all the time.'

'But what *can* I do?'

'You can tell people your story, so they know how these battles can be won. Or, you could do another petition?' Bracewell suggested. 'Right now, you are the reluctant poster boy for exposing corruption, believe it or not.'

'Whatever it takes,' I said.

Juliette put her hand on mine. 'No, Ben,' she said. 'Enough is enough. I am not bringing the world into these four walls. We need to move on with our life.'

TWENTY-SIX

CHRISTINE WAS WAITING, as we agreed, at five on the dot, outside the tobacconist at the station.

I had expected a more tired version of the lithe, stylish woman that Juliette and I had first met. But, perhaps mindful of what she was here to do, Christine was dressed in a tight Karen Millen suit, thin black piping accentuating her honed curves. Her face, only lightly touched with makeup, shone with optimism. Her whole demeanour suggested better ways of living.

When she sensed me approach behind her Christine turned and greeted me with a coquettish smile, her chin against her shoulder. Her dark hair fanned gracefully over her chest. We exchanged quick kisses on the cheek, and moved into a patisserie nearby.

In it, dark-eyed waitresses thumbed Penguin paperbacks behind the counter. My eyes were drawn by glass domes filled with rich sponge cakes. But I knew my best friends former girlfriend well enough to know that at this time of the afternoon, in fitting with her cultural aspirations, she liked to have an espresso. So I ordered one for both of us.

Christine politely enquired about Juliette, but I had one eye on a carefully planned schedule. 'Phillip's talk ends in just over one hour,' I said. 'And he's getting the 19.20 from Platform One home.'

'Okay,' she said, raising the cup. Her expression betrayed months of doubt. Behind her elegant veneer I sensed a wasteland of private recrimination.

'Don't worry,' I said. 'He is keen to make amends with you. But you know Phillip. He isn't sure how to make the first step.'

'He knows how to make all the steps after it,' she said.

I laughed. 'Just be on the platform, shoot him a smile, and I assure you he will do the rest.'

She smiled. It was bruised, at once melancholy, and hopeful. 'What are you two like? You don't have a kind word to say to each other's faces, but behind the scenes you're devoted to each other.'

I thought darkly of Violet. How I needed this ruse to work, in order to keep our friendship. 'Believe me, this is the least I can do,' I said.

'You're a good friend,' she said.

I glanced at my watch, and decided that I needed to make my apologies, and leave.

The hotel had a sense of opulence that I was unused to. As I waited for Phillip, in its expansive lobby, I looked up at a sparkling chandelier. The sign outside the events room, just in my eyeline, boasted a famous set of names for a conference on 'Advancements in Entertainment'. No one had been more surprised than Phillip when his request to speak at it was accepted. It wouldn't start for a few more minutes. Although the attendants were already inside, Phillip had been adamant that he didn't want to mix with what he mock-imperiously called 'his public' before he spoke.

'I should never have allowed myself to be talked into this,' Phillip said, advancing towards me from the reception. 'I've done enough for you already.' I noticed he was wearing a crumpled navy suit.

'Is Art coming today?' I asked.

'Probably. You should hang around for him. There's still plenty of money to be made out of your name, now.'

'That whole accusation, about me getting paid for the talk show appearance nearly derailed my case at the hearing. Art stitched me right up.'

'Yeah, but that appearance paid for Bracewell,' Phillip said.

'Right,' I said, looking at my watch. 'I'm getting the lift upstairs. They'll be finishing in a couple of minutes.'

'Best of British,' Phillip said, heading towards the events room.

The conference on the top floor, in a more lavish ballroom, advertised a day of debate about 'Moral Leadership in Teaching.' The sign outside the ballroom had described Paul Kraver as a keynote speaker, speaking on the final panel of the day, about 'how to run a school with impeccable business ethics'.

The door was ajar, and as I peered in through the crack I could see Kraver, walking up and down in front of an audience seated at circular tables. He was strutting in the same way he had on his first day at Cranley Wood.

'There is a very simple way to ensure your leadership always has integrity,' he was saying. 'You're thinking "it must be so complicated", but I'm here to tell you, no, no, no, it couldn't be simpler. You just need to be an honest person. Sometimes it can be a risk, in this world, to be honest. Yes, people will exploit you. But, by staying on the true path, step by step, you make the workplace a happy environment.'

As the long hand on my watch moved close to quarter-to-six he wound his speech up, and I took a few steps back as the delegates started to congregate, sticky platelets around the open vessel of the entrance. They coagulated around the free coffee and croissants, exchanging compliments, numbers and subtle claims about status. The lift was opposite the entrance, and I lingered by the side of it, my back to the ballroom, as the people streamed out.

I saw Paul Kraver, from the side of my eyes, before he saw me.

He walked out of the ballroom, strode past the refreshments, and made straight for the lift. I turned so he wouldn't see me, as he pushed the gold button to call the lift. It felt like a lifetime of furtive glances passed before it arrived, but somehow he didn't notice me there. I exhaled as the lift announced its arrival with a ping. As I moved to join him in it I reached into my left jacket pocket, to call Phillip, whose name was waiting on the screen of my mobile. I quickly put a hand into my right pocket, and pressed a button on the device in there too.

The lifts were just beginning to close when he turned in the lift, and saw that the two of us, for the next few moments, would be trapped together.

I somehow knew this would be our final joust. In every one we'd had, he had always destroyed me. He had responded to every swing from me by hitting me harder than I could imagine. This time, I was determined to land at least one punch. I had played this scenario through in my head many times, preparing for him just as I had imagined he had often prepared for me.

'Well, I can only wonder what you're doing here,' he said, as the lift jolted into action.

'You must think of me as a nagging pain that won't go away,' I said, stepping closer to him. He inched backwards.

There was a moment in which we eyed each other's pound of flesh, and wondered how a fight might end. In a flash I decided that I was the most physically agile, but he was the more substantial. I would move quickly, and hope that a jab caused invisible damage.

He would bide his time to make a killer blow, one with all his weight behind it. In his eyes I could see a sudden wager going on, but it seemed more mental than physical. He raised his nose.

'It's quite the contrary in fact,' he said. 'I always had you right where I wanted you. I'm still here, aren't I?'

He leant back on the rail as the lift whirred.

'Only because you had no problem lying to the police, lying to the school, and digging up every bit of dirt you could on me.'

I got a dark rush I'd never had before. These seconds will count, I thought. In the grand scheme of my life, these seconds will count.

'Yes, yes,' he said, with a smile. 'But you're forgetting one thing though, aren't you? I didn't dig up dirt on you. You created dirt about yourself, by carrying on with that floozy. All I had to do was hire someone to get proof. But you went public with your grievance so clumsily that I had plenty to use against you, didn't I?'

'How could you do it?' I asked, stepping even closer. His eyes snapped to the side. 'You knew that Marine had been unlawfully killed, that Walker should never have been employed.'

'You think everything's personal,' he hissed. 'You can't blame a lion for tearing apart a gazelle. It's nature, isn't it?'

'It isn't natural, or right, to lie to the police. You seemed pretty good at getting them to look at exactly what you wanted them to see – and nothing else.'

'You don't get to run three schools without having some friends in high places. But you wouldn't know that, having never got off the first rung.'

'Bribery?'

'Let's just say I know a police inspector who has a few little secrets he wouldn't want splashed about in the papers. I found that was enough to slow you down.'

'So you knew Walker was guilty, and you still allowed him to supervise the children at the school?'

'Might as well be hung for a sheep than a lamb, that's what my Dad always said. Or in my case, not hung at all.'

'You're not as clever as you think,' I said, as the lift began to slow. 'The public knows, the parents know, and the staff know. One more slip-up and you'll not only be sacked by the school, but you will never be employed again.'

'No, you see, wrong again,' he said, wagging a finger. 'Not while I have the board of governors in my pocket. What you don't realize is that I stay a few moves ahead. Even now, I'm a few moves ahead of you. I let people think they are dictating the game, but it's all a part of the fun for me.' The lift whirred to a standstill. 'It's the one thing you never did work out, you or your little team of money-grabbers. How exactly did I manage to prevent those governors from sacking me?'

'Go on.' I said.

The lift stopped. My time had run out. I would never know.

He drew closer to me. His eyes were bloodshot as he spat the words in my face. 'Knowing a few secrets is more than enough to keep people working for you. Oooh, they'll work harder than they've ever worked for themselves, you mark my words. But I'm not that daft,' he said, looking me up and down. 'If I tell you any more, you might be able to get me.'

The doors opened. He shook his head. 'Out of my way,' he said, pushing past.

People got in, and lined the sides of the lift. Kraver, a few steps outside, turned to face me with a small smile. As I held his gaze I put a hand in my pocket, pulled out a whirring Dictaphone and lifted it up for him. As the lift doors began to shut I watched his smile fall.

The lift began its ascent up the building again. I reached into my other pocket, smiling at the woman next to me, and I pulled out my mobile phone. The phone call to Phillip was still active. 'You get all that?' I said, fearing for my signal as the lift moved.

'I can't believe you got him to say all that so quickly,' Phillip said, through a cloud of feedback. 'You've got more than enough to get him convicted.'

When I met him in the lobby, Phillip looked exhilarated.

'I thought you might coax him into one or two indiscretions,' he said. 'But you struck gold.'

'I think, in his own way, he thought he was getting revenge on me,' I said, looking around to check who was listening. Various people were lingering at the reception.

'So he has some dirt on a police officer, and a school governor,' Phillip said. 'With your profile, I reckon you can blow the lid off the whole arrangement,' he said.

'I have no interest in doing that,' I said. 'But with this on tape I think I can finally get Kraver sacked. Perhaps I'll have to strike a deal with someone, let them know that I am ready to share this recording with the world, and have other people ready to do that too if anything happens to me or mine. Two can play at Kraver's game.'

'Be careful,' he said. 'You don't want to get your hands too dirty.'

'You're right,' I said. 'I want just enough mud on my hands that some of it sticks to him. Then, it's time to move on.'

Phillip nodded. 'You need to get out, before he finds you. I'll let you know how the talk goes. We pulled that off pretty well in the end, didn't we?' he said, placing his hand on my shoulder.

'Thanks to your help.'

'You owe me,' he said.

'I know,' I answered.

TWENTY-SEVEN

I CAREFULLY PLANNED the moment I would play my recording to Kraver down the phone. I made sure my message was left too late on a Friday afternoon for him to pick it up that day. Ensuring he would hear the fuzzy sound of his own confession, captured on a Dictaphone, on an answerphone message early on a Monday morning. Once I had played the recording in full I left my telephone number. 'Perhaps you should call me,' I said.

He phoned me at 9 a.m, on the following Monday. Our conversation was brief and terse. 'So what do you want?' he asked.

'I want this job to be your last,' I said. 'No more positions outside your role as headmaster. You give all of them up, and you coast straight towards an early retirement. If you don't, then I will make sure that lots of people get a copy of our conversation. Which would lead not only to you getting sacked, but arrested. You'll be all over the news, and any position you have held onto will just generate more negative publicity for you.'

'Fine,' he said.

It was just one word. But it was said with enough venom, that I knew for once I was a move ahead of him. At last I felt able to let the matter go.

As time went on I heard various stories about Kraver, slavishly repeated to me by friends and acquaintances. Stories in which people confronted him over his handling of Marine's case, on many occasions. Something about his lack of remorse, or acceptance, only made people more determined to leave a mark on him. The impression I got was that Kraver grew increasingly defensive and bitter. I realized that people like him had no sincere relationship with the truth. To him honesty, morality and truth were just ideas, ideas that only interested him when they could be used as instruments. It was a mindset that had given him benefits in the short term, particularly in our short-term world. But this attitude had cost him in the long term. Like other corrupt people, he would never realize that his punishment was in missing out on what he didn't know he could have. I doubt his money was enough of a balm to truly soothe him.

My encounter with him in the lift had confirmed something to me. People never fully confront their wrongdoing. They are all trying to push for their own ends, and they lack the strength to truly apologise for that. In my heart of hearts, I wondered if I was just the same. However different I thought I was to Kraver, I too was called to account, on regular occasions, for the mistakes I had made.

The secrets Kraver used to keep himself in power were never revealed. I stopped checking up on him, after a while. I had a new job to focus on, in a new school, where there were no reminders of a painful past.

None of that means that the loose ends in my head were completely tied up. Or that the liminal, nightly landscape Juliette had found herself marooned in was left behind. I found ways to cope with Marine's death, even if the world largely seemed to now consider the matter closed. Juliette and I confided in one another, about the mistakes we had made during that time, and we both found ways to draw a line in the sand. In a way, we found a closeness that we had never had before we went through this ordeal together. It gave me the confidence to finally propose to her, and a few months after she accepted we had a small wedding in a local church. On a spring day when the blossoms mixed with confetti in the warm, enticing air. That day she held my hand more firmly than she ever had, and even though I knew the complications in our relationship would not end there I knew we would at least share them from now on. I even told Juliette about the day, two years after the enquiry concluded, that I bumped into Violet.

I had not responded to the messages of congratulation Violet texted me after the case hit the papers. I assumed she would understand that I now needed to focus on my relationship, or even that I had suspicions about her having been recruited to damage it. I never was able to quite acknowledge that Violet possibly could have served such a function. I decided that it was a paranoid concern, which did not equate with the Violet I knew. With the young woman, bursting with potential, who had rescued me on the night that I had been ready to throw myself off a bridge.

I ran into her whilst walking to a squash match at the university sport centre. I spotted her in the distance, a mythical presence at the other end of the plaza. Her downy movements imbued by the distinct fuzz of her consciousness.

My first assumption was that she had planned for this to happen. But the sheer surprise on her face proved that was not the case.

'Ben,' she said. 'How on earth have you been?'

She seemed more confident, more refined. The bright student colours had been shed, in favour of subtle shades of cream.

'I'm okay,' I said. 'I've been well. And you?'

'They've given me a couple of modules to teach at the uni,' she said, 'so I was finally able to get myself decked out. I've gone up in the world like you wouldn't believe.'

'That's brilliant. Listen, I am so sorry that I didn't reply to your messages.'

She looked at the floor. 'I didn't have a phone for a few months anyway,' she said, her voice bizarrely taking on a slight Cockney accent. 'But yeah, I did notice that you didn't get in touch. I had assumed you needed to re-build things at home. That having me around wouldn't have been a great help.'

'That's true,' I said, 'but I still should have thanked you. It's just that something made me suspicious.'

I explained about the photos.

I wasn't sure how to interpret her expression as I told the story. Violet looked morbidly curious, rather than guilty.

'In that case I can completely understand why you didn't reply,' she said, reacting quickly.

'I know it's stupid. But I couldn't help but wonder about the final photo in the envelope. Where you seemed to be looking straight at the camera.'

'Now you mention it,' she said, pushing a strand of hair from her face, 'I know this sounds really strange, but I did think I saw someone in the bushes that night.'

'I don't remember that.'

'I said something to you about it, don't you remember? I'm wondering now if that was the moment the photo was taken. As we opened the door. You have to believe me – if I was looking right at the camera it is purely by accident.'

I took her elbow and for a moment that familiar pulse of blood, whenever we made contact, dizzied me. 'Of course I believe you,' I said. 'You came into my life when I was at my very lowest ebb and you saved me from…I don't know what. Oblivion!'

She couldn't help but laugh. 'Oblivion!' she said. 'I'm sure that's not the case, Ben.'

'I don't know how I ever doubted you. You gave me inspiration when I most needed it. And those tweets you wrote on my behalf - I hear they were Favourited a thousand times.'

'That is true,' she said, nodding. 'I'm glad that in some ways I helped. Although, there is something that I would like to tell you.'

I waited, as a couple of students in tie-dyed shirts lingered behind us, exchanging phone numbers.

'What?' I asked. 'You've got me worried now.'

'I didn't tell you, because it was the night before your enquiry. But I did get a very strange phone call. From someone claiming to be a detective.'

'Did he give a name?'

'No. And that made it hard to get the conversation off the ground! But he did tell me he was working for a very powerful "organisation" – that was his word – and that he had a business proposition for me. I thought it was some dodgy overseas college wanting cheap lecturers!'

'Go on.'

'Well, he said he knew I was close to you, and that they had reason to believe I could offer them some valuable information. Mentioned something about how it would be "for the greater good". The guy just said how I could "surely do with the money", and he seemed to know how little I was earning. Obviously, I turned him down. But I was genuinely worried for a few days that they were going to exhort me. Or have me expelled from the university.'

'Jesus.'

'I know,' she said, rubbing her face. 'I had a few sleepless nights, wondering if all the work I'd done to make something of myself would be for nothing if they decided to make something up.'

I saw remembered pain etch onto her face.

'I'm so sorry, Violet. So what exactly did you say to them?'

'I just told them I couldn't do it, and then I threw away my phone!'

'And they never bothered you again?'

'How could they?' she said, with a small smile.

'I should go,' I said. 'It won't do my relationship any good if more photos come through of me touching your arm.'

'Ben, no one is going to be following you now,' she said. 'You do know that?'

'I know,' I said. 'It's just that whole fight…it sometimes makes me paranoid.'

'I can understand that,' she said, looking past me.

'Just before I go …' I stopped myself.

'What is it Ben?'

I winced.

'Come on, you must know you can tell me. I kept everything else to myself!'

'Of course. I know it's possibly borderline weird, as I was attached, with a child and you're, well, much younger than I am...'

'Not that much younger,' she said, cocking her head to one side.

'Sure. It's just - whatever we had, it was important to me. More than I can say.'

'It's amazing to hear you say that,' she said. She looked around her, before dropping her voice to a whisper. 'The period of time, when we were in each other's lives, really shaped me. I learnt so much from how you handled it.'

'Take care, Violet,' I said.

I took in the small smile, the hunched shoulders, and that distinct, elusive scent, one last time.

TWENTY-EIGHT

DESPITE JULIETTE and I rediscovering our sense of intimacy, my grief did harden into a personal ritual. A ritual that I entered into on occasional, solitary weekends on the coast. At the beach that I had once taken my new family to, during our first weekend away.

To my mind, everything that surrounds that hallowed beach is a kind of magical apparatus.

On the journey there I was struck by how mundane objects, from the steel gantry leading onto the ferry, to the salt-encrusted windows revealing the glacial sea on-board, were each instilled with a cool potency. It made me shiver in anticipation to walk through the process of finding that beach. During that trip it occurred to me that by savouring these rituals, which took me to the place where I saw Marine flourish, I was stepping through my own phantasmagoria. Into the crystalline world of my own psyche, whose architecture was enshrined in permanence, no matter how much the real world changed.

I sleepwalked onto the ferry, down the pier on the other side to the shore, into the taxi to the bed and breakfast. Once there I found a temporary home in a sparsely decorated, sunlit room high above the sea, and then on that beach. In this place I was finally able to use the mystical, shifting matter of my own memory to convince myself that Marine still existed in a loop of time. On a slip of beautiful, private, ribbon. At once so fragile and so strong that no nightmarish events could ever damage that spool.

Throughout the preparatory rituals to get to that beach, I acted like a normal man. At the bed and breakfast, my friendliness seemed slightly laced with a desperation to please. Whilst devouring a hearty breakfast. I did my very best to let the signals of my body language say 'all is normal'. Even as I stepped outside, approaching where my delicate, milk-skinned Marine once played, I looked to all the world like a normal, middle-aged man – lonely perhaps, but certainly curious. But, like a guardian of my own mythology, I knew that at every step I would keep the importance, the hunger, the almost religious quality of this inner ceremony a secret. I was stepping into my own internal landscape, and the act itself was too potent for me to even fear being disturbed. I needed it; it revived and invigorated me.

As I walked towards the cool beach on that quiet day I realized that Juliette had been undertaking a similar ritual whilst singing 'La Clare De La Lune' to herself. Juliette had, in fact, entered her own crepuscular world earlier than me, and its topography was very different. Where mine was sandy, with a hint of salt in the air, and the churn of the sea in the background, hers was luminescent, and based around the idea of a beautiful moon being. Juliette's inner world was accessed through music, melody, and memory. Mine required the subtle hoots of early morning hours, the crisp walk down to the deserted sand, the long canvas of a distant horizon on which my imagination could draw. I needed space to

AN HONEST DECEIT

unfurl this ritual, and enough peace to discipline my mind as it required.

I walked, on a beautiful and solitary morning, out of the bed and breakfast, and across its gravelled driveway. I looked back at the hunched, grey stone building, set in a small copse. I stepped up a sparsely grassed mount, the ascent of which led me to a row of trees silhouetted against a white morning sea. I walked down to the shingle, where the sea rose to me like a strong friend, with shoulders too broad for the embrace it deserved. My landscape became musical too, as I recalled the saccharine, haunting melody of the Celine Dion song that Juliette hummed that weekend. Even the concrete slope down to the gold slip of the beach was magical turf. I walked to the rowing boat, powder blue, slightly too small for a man of my age, that the proprietor of the bed and breakfast owned. I tugged it down to the surf, the sea's lachrymose lap a tender embrace at my too-white feet. I pushed the vessel onto the bobbing waves, and kicked my shoes into the sandy hull. The eggshell interior, and the white sun overhead, all delicately welcomed me. The sun cleansed the world.

I slipped the sandy oars into the rowlocks, assumed the position on the seat. I squinted at the exquisite pain of the early morning sun. As the oars splashed in the sea I was splashing into paradise. Not because I had, through any sense of discipline, absorbed the psychic landscape in which I intended to seek Marine. But because I was staving off that moment, like a connoisseur, so I could open it at my own choosing. I knew that this scene, and my mind, would allow that moment to occur in time, and that when it happened it would be exquisite.

For now, I pushed the oars into the clear, splashing aqua, and I pointed my little boat out towards a distant horizon. I knew I would never reach it, and the thought was as romantic as Marine's thoughts might have been as she sat, enchanted by the possibilities of an open sea. When I was far enough out I pulled the oars back into the hull and I kicked back, and laid my body taut between the two seating panels. I placed my hands carefully behind my head. The boat took on every nuance and contour of the sea, and I let its motions dissolve through me.

The sunlight overhead was so white, so heavenly, that its caress almost forced my eyes open. When it did, I turned to the water. It was clear, and blue, and, like a child's submerged hair, seaweed splayed on the sunlit surface. I let my hand roll in the cool water. I felt the chill of expectation, the soothing effect of the calm waves. The pleasure that came with the promise of a never-ending horizon I was perpetually floating towards.

I eventually did return to the sand. I pulled the little boat back into its place, and made my way up the beach, to the sea wall. When I turned, I saw that there was a dinghy by the shore, just like the one Marine had hidden behind all those years ago. I sat fifteen yards from it, so it was directly in front of me, barely daring to catch my breath. I closed my eyes. The moment was coming. I savoured it, and let it roll. Soon, wonderfully soon, I was ready. I listened to the sea. When I opened me eyes, sure enough, Marine was there. Peeking round at me from behind that little boat, her little nose decorated with freckles.

'Daddy,' she was saying. 'Daddy. Where do fish go in the winter?'

I didn't hurry to close my eyes. I took her in. Soft, full of promise, her hair full of sunlight. My daughter.

When I closed my eyes I realized my face was wet with tears.

AN HONEST DECEIT

Acknowledgements

THIS NOVEL WAS researched using a Grant for the Arts which was offered by the Arts Council UK. I'd like to thank the team at the Arts Council who were helpful and accommodating at every turn. Their funding allowed me to interview experts on corruption, such as Andrew Jennings, who offered me compelling insights into the practices at FIFA in the months before that scandal broke.

This book also benefited from the insights into corruption offered by other high-profile whistle-blowers, Paul Moore and David Drew.

Special thanks to Jonathan Smith. As a legal advisor, second to none, and one of the few friends who insist on giving more than they take.

I would like to thank Matthew at Urbane Publications for taking this novel on. This novel has evolved a lot in the five years since it was conceived and it was good to finally find a home for it with Urbane.

GUY MANKOWSKI is a journalist, academic and author. His debut novel, *The Intimates*, was a New Writing North Recommended Read in 2011. His second novel, *Letters from Yelena*, was adapted for the stage and Osiris Educational used an extract of it in GCSE training material. His third novel, *How I Left The National Grid*, was written as part of a PhD in Creative Writing at Northumbria University.